INTERNET for KIDS!

A Beginner's Guide to Surfing the Net

Written by Ted Pedersen and Francis Moss

This book is designed primarily for
Windows™ -based and Macintosh™ systems.

Where to go online for more cool Internet information:

The Putnam Berkley Group offers a list of books available at:

http://www.putnam.com

For more information about Price Stern Sloan and its complete line of books,
our e-mail address is:

pssbooks.com

And the MCA/Universal Cyberwalk World Wide Web site
has fun entertainment and information:

http://www.mca.com

Editor: Lisa Rojany
Assistant Editors: Daniel Weizmann and Michi Fujimoto
Art Director: Sheena Needham
Illustrator: Valerie Costantino
Book Designer: Beth Bender

Text copyright © 1995 Ted Pedersen and Francis Moss
Illustrations copyright © 1995 Price Stern Sloan, Inc.
The terms **CyberSarge** and **Cyberspace Academy** are integral to the
copyrighted content of this text and are © 1995 Ted Pedersen and Francis Moss
Published by Price Stern Sloan, Inc.,
A member of The Putnam & Grosset Group,
New York, New York.

Library of Congress Cataloging-in-Publication Data

Pedersen, Ted.
Internet for kids: a beginner's guide to surfing the Net / written by Ted Pedersen and Francis Moss.
p. cm.
Summary: Introduces the computer network known as the Internet, providing step-by-step instructions, sample projects, lists of boards to join, and a parents' guide to protect against possible negative aspects of the Internet.
ISBN 0-8431-3957-9
1. Internet (Computer network)—Juvenile literature.
[1. Internet (Computer network) 2. Computers.] I. Moss, Francis.
II. Title.
TK5105.875.I57P43 1995
004.6'7—dc20   5-11435
                                               CIP
                                          AC

First Edition   ISBN 0-8431-3957-9
10 9 8 7 6 5 4 3 2 1

DEDICATION

For Phyllis and Phyllis,
and for Caitlin and Zach,
and all the other kids,
no matter what their age,
who'll be cruising the Net
into the 21st Century.

:-) :) :-o :-! :-' :-D :*) :-p (:-& :-" :-(

TABLE OF CONTENTS

Introduction **1**

Tales of the Internet:
What a Typical Internet Experience Might Be Like **5**

PART I

Cadet: Welcome to Cyberspace Academy **15**

Chapter 1
Life on the Internet: What's It All About? **23**

Chapter 2
Preparing for Liftoff: How Do I Get Online? **41**

Chapter 3
Pilot's Manual for the Internet: What Do I Do Once I Get Online? **51**

Chapter 4
Navigating the Internet: How Do I Get Around in Cyberspace? **87**

PART II

Explorer: Living in Cyberspace **99**

Chapter 5
The Top Ten Rules for Surfing the Net **101**

Chapter 6
Keeping Your Internet Log Plus 12 Logs to Get You Started! **107**

Chapter 7
Guide to the Galaxy:Cool Places to Surf on the Net **117**

PART III

Commander: Welcome Parents and Teachers **149**

Chapter 8
Finding your Cybership: Choosing an Online Company or Service Provider . . **151**

Chapter 9
Recording Your Internet Gateway Information Plus 4 Charts to Personalize . . **161**

Chapter 10
Parents' Guide: Where Are Your Kids Tonight on the Internet?
Plus an Official Internet Contract for Parents and Kids **167**

Chapter 11
Glossary: More Technical (But Fun!) Terms You Might Come Across **175**

Index of Terms **199**

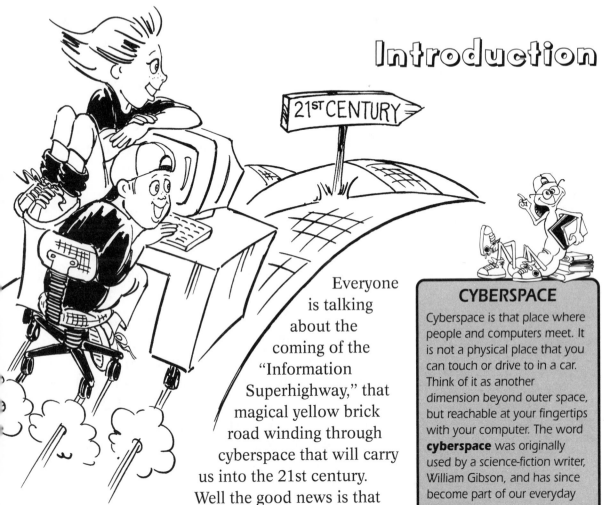

Introduction

Everyone is talking about the coming of the "Information Superhighway," that magical yellow brick road winding through cyberspace that will carry us into the 21st century. Well the good news is that the Information Superhighway is here already, and it's called the *Internet*. The bad news is that it's like some of the streets in our big cities, full of detours, potholes, and unmarked off ramps. In other words, there's a lot to be found on the Internet, but finding it can sometimes be tough.

Finding a place on the Internet is a lot like finding a house in Tokyo, where all the addresses in a neighborhood are assigned by when a house was

CYBERSPACE

Cyberspace is that place where people and computers meet. It is not a physical place that you can touch or drive to in a car. Think of it as another dimension beyond outer space, but reachable at your fingertips with your computer. The word **cyberspace** was originally used by a science-fiction writer, William Gibson, and has since become part of our everyday language.

NOTE TO READERS:

Whenever you come across a word you don't understand, just check the Glossary, starting on page 175. If you need to refer back to a particular section of the book where a term is discussed in more detail, check the Index of Terms, starting on page 199.

built, rather than where it is located on the street. You really need a guide to get around in Tokyo—or to surf the Internet.

There are a lot of books about the Internet. Some of them are better than others. But none of them have been written for the audience that is going to be most affected by the Internet—you!

It is kids like yourself who are going to have to navigate through this exciting and fascinating landscape of cyberspace in order to prepare for the 21st Century.

That's what this book is all about.

It's all about piloting your own cybership and traveling at warp speeds through an uncharted universe of fun, games, and information. In other words, going where no kid has gone before.

Throughout this book we provide instructions on how to get online, what to do once you get there, suggestions about where to go in cyberspace, choosing an online service, and definitions of new and technical terms which you can find at the sides of the main body of text, in the Glossary, and in the Index of Terms. Whenever you see a **CyberSarge Says,** you'll get handy pieces of advice about surfing the Net, not to mention all the charts to personalize, logs, and note sheets we give you so you can jot down everything you learn.

No matter how thorough and up-to-date we've attempted to be, cyberspace changes daily. New people, sites, and businesses go online every day. We have not been able to include every site on the Internet nor information about every service provider. Those would be guide books in themselves and defeat the purpose of this one, which is to

INTERNET

The Internet is simply a network of computers all hooked up together and talking to one another. Once you get on the Internet, you will be able to send electronic mail to your friends—no matter where in the world they live, read bulletin boards, travel in cyberspace on an information superhighway called **the Web,** and so much more! We'll tell you all about the Internet in this book!

provide a simple, easy-to-understand guide for children. In addition, the rate charts and list of services offered may change without notice.

As such, we have recommended Internet sites and services that exist at the time of this book's publication. We expect most of them to exist in the future, but there are no guarantees—cyberspace is a living entity, developing and changing even as you read this. We have taken pains to insure the accuracy of all the information in this guide; yet despite the best efforts of everyone involved, an error may occur from time to time. As editors and publishers, we at Price Stern Sloan take pride in our work, but we cannot take responsibility for errors that might occur. However, we certainly value your input. If you note an error, please write to us: Editors of Internet for Kids/Price Stern Sloan, Inc., c/o The Putnam & Grosset Group, 200 Madison Avenue, New York, NY 10016. We will investigate and attempt to revise our entry where indicated. In the meantime, enjoy your Internet travels, and take notes for yourself in the recording logs and note sheets we provide.

But we're jumping ahead. We'll let you discover the Internet at an easy pace as you make that leap into cyberspace.

Welcome to the future.

Tales of the Internet:

What a Typical Internet Experience Might Be Like

Meet Kate. That's short for Kaitlin. Kate's a red-headed, blue-eyed 7th grader at Hillside Middle School in California.

Kate was like you just a short while ago. She had heard about the Internet but didn't really know much about it. Eager to find out, she read this book from cover to cover. When she finished, she knew everything she needed to know. Now she's a pro!

So if you'd like to see what life on the Internet is like for her now that she knows what it's all about, come join us. We're about to embark on a journey to the world of cyberspace! And don't worry: If you don't understand some of the words in this section, everything will be explained later on. This is just a little introduction so that you can get a taste of what life is like in cyberspace!

This is what a typical day is like for Kate.

It's 2:00 P.M. Monday. Kate arrives home from school, puts her books on her desk in her room, and turns on her computer.

"Ready for takeoff," Kate says to herself as the computer beeps, announcing that it's ready for work.

Phyllis, Kate's mom, comes into her room. "Hi, hon," she says. "Got homework to do?"

"Yep. A bunch," Kate replies. "I've got a book report due for English, and I promised my science teacher I'd find her some pictures of the comets hitting Jupiter."

"Sounds like you'll be busy this afternoon," Phyllis says.

"Not only that, I haven't chatted with Elise, my friend in Paris, for nearly a month," Kate says.

"Can I add one more thing to your list?" Kate's mom asks. "I need an idea of what to cook for dinner. I've got broccoli and chicken, and nothing in my cookbooks sounds interesting."

"No problem," Kate says as she maneuvers a pointing device—called a mouse—attached to her computer.

Kate has a software program that allows her to connect her computer to the Internet. Kate recently learned how this works: Using her computer, she telephones a bigger computer in her hometown that's connected to another computer, which is connected to still *another* computer, and so on. These connected computers, all over the world, make up the Internet. The Internet is referred to in many different ways including: "a network of networks," and the "Information Superhighway."

Kate's computer signals her that it's connected—or logged on—to the

Internet. She types in her password. Don't look over her shoulder! Her password is hers alone, and she doesn't share it with anyone, not even her best friend, Audrey.

Kate decides to read the electronic mail messages that other people have sent her. On her computer, she starts up a special mail program that finds out if there is any e-mail waiting for her.

As she does this, Kate keeps an eye on the clock. Time on the Internet costs money, so she and her parents have agreed that her use of the Internet is limited to a few hours a week.

Kate finds a message there from a friend she knows only by her handle—that's like a nickname—"Turtle." Turtle lives all the way across the United States in New Jersey. Kate reads the message, smiling at the joke Turtle tells:

> A science teacher comes home exhausted and complaining of a headache.
> His wife asks: "What's the matter?"
> The science teacher replies: "Our computer at school broke down and I had to think!"

Kate thinks of a joke to send to Turtle and begins to write a reply.

Kate glances at the clock again. Because she is allowed only a certain amount of time per day, she thinks that maybe she should disconnect—or go offline—from the Internet and reply offline, so as not to use up her time. By disconnecting from the Internet, writing her reply, and then reconnecting to send her message, she can save time. But it's too much trouble to go offline for one message. Besides, her mom would probably agree that hunting recipes and doing homework don't really count against her online time anyway—right? Kate jots down a note to herself to remember to talk to her mom about these time-allowed details; they have agreed to touch base whenever Kate has a question.

Back at her computer again, Kate sends Turtle her own joke:

What's green and slimy, with three eyes and ten legs?
I don't know.
I don't know either, but they're serving it for lunch in the cafeteria!

Now Kate decides to take care of her mom's request and begins her search of the Internet for a recipe. She knows that several computers on the Internet have files of recipes. By connecting her computer to one of these, she can search for recipes that contain both broccoli and chicken. Within seconds she's gotten several recipes, plus the name of a discussion group that publishes hundreds of recipes. She writes down the name of the discussion group in her Internet log, then tells her computer to copy the recipes and print them out on her printer. Kate runs into the kitchen with the recipe printout.

Phyllis nods as she glances over the recipes. "Thanks, Kate," she tells her daughter. "I'll use one of these recipes tonight and see how it comes out!"

Back in her room, Kate wonders whether she should do her homework or check her e-mail again. She hopes to find a message from Elise in Paris, who promised Kate she'd be in touch this week.

Kate glances at her clock. It's 11:30 at night in Paris. Elise stays up late studying a lot, but she's probably already in bed. Just in case, Kate opens her e-mail program. Rats! No mail. Just as she's about to quit the program, there's a musical *ding*! from her computer. More e-mail is coming in! Kate reads the message header, a line at the top of the e-mail page that identifies who the sender of the message is. It's from Elise!

Kate reads the message:

> "Ma **chére chât**, my dear cat . . ."

This greeting is Elise's joke on Kate's name (*chât* means *cat* in French).

Elise continues:

> "I will be at our usual place on the Internet at 3:00 P.M., your time, so we can have a discussion online. Sorry to post this so late, but I just finished studying. I hope you receive it in time. **Tout à l'heure**, see you soon. **Ton amie**, your friend, Elise."

Kate looks at her clock. It's now 2:30 P.M. She decides to finish her homework. She uses a special software program called a *Web browser* to search the World Wide Web. The Web is on the Internet. It is the home of some of the most interesting parts of the Internet. The Web is a library, supermarket, museum, research tool, idea trove, game room, and art gallery—all rolled into one! It has tens of thousands—maybe even hundreds of thousands!—of locations to visit with useful and interesting information.

By typing in the phrase **Shoemaker-Levy**, the name of the comet that crashed into Jupiter, Kate locates a computer at the University of Arizona that has pictures of the comet she's looking for.

Kate calls up the University of Arizona at the following Internet address: *seds.lpl.arizona.edu*. After a brief search, she finds several computerized images of Shoemaker-

Levy fragments hitting Jupiter. She chooses the three she likes best and copies them onto her computer. Then she prints them out on her printer. She smiles to herself, knowing that this will get her some points with her teacher!

By the time Kate has finished with the comet, it's almost 3:00 P.M.—time for Elise to connect online with her! Kate loads up another software program that connects her with the Internet Relay Chat, or IRC, network. This network allows her to *chat*—or talk—online with her friend in France—all for the cost of a local phone call! Kate finds the private channel she and Elise share. A channel is like a room where you can chat with as many or as few people as you wish.

Kate sees the words appear on her screen as Elise is typing them:

"Hello, Kate . . ."

Kate would rather chat with Elise in private, so we'll leave her for now. We'll drop by Grant Elementary School, where Kate's little brother, Zack, is working after classes in the school's computer lab.

Although younger than his sister—he's nine years old—Zack shares her blue eyes and freckles, as well as her love of computers. He is pretty good at this computer stuff, too. Their father, Frank, is a plumber who got both of his children interested in computers when he started using one to keep track of his customers, his suppliers, and his bills. Zack remembers that when he and Kate were younger, they would sit with their father while he worked on the computer. When Frank was finished with his work, he'd load up a computer game they could all play.

Now Zack stays after school in the computer lab twice a week to help his teacher keep the lab clean and get the computers ready for the next day's classes. In return, his teacher lets Zack spend some time exploring (Zack and his teacher call it *surfing*) the Internet.

Today Zack has some homework to do, too. His class just finished reading *Tom Sawyer*, by Mark Twain. He's got a report due on the author, and his school library doesn't have the books he needs to do research about life on the Mississippi River during Tom Sawyer's time. Zack thinks that the main branch of his local library might have the books, but the staff there is often too busy to look up the books for him.

Zack connects his school's computer to a remote computer—one that is connected to *his* computer through the phone lines—at a university in another state, and finds his local library's card catalog there. He can actually tell if the books are checked out or not! He sees that his local library has two copies of one of the books he's looking for. Chances are when he goes to his local library tomorrow after school, he'll find the book. Using the Internet, he just saved himself a lot of time!

Now it's Zack's favorite time—playing a MUD. That stands for *Multiple User Dimensions*. MUDs are Internet-based games that many players, on computers anywhere in the world, can all play at once. Zack is playing a MUD started by kids his own age! He follows the instructions, and soon he's typing in commands for his online character—his very own game player that he uses while on the Internet—to follow.

Zack plays for half an hour. Then his e-mail program beeps at him. Zack pauses his game, then reads the message. It's from Kate.

"Time to come home for dinner, little brother."

With a sigh, Zack quits the game and signs off the Net (short for *Internet*). He waves goodbye to his teacher as he heads for home. He hates to end an adventure in cyberspace so early. Wouldn't you? If you knew what you were missing, you sure would! But before you can do what Kate and Zack do in this section, you need to learn everything that they did. If you're ready to do just that, read on!

PART 1

Cadet:

Welcome to Cyberspace Academy

It's time to get started. Buckle up. Turn on your computer. You're about to leap into an amazing place. It's called Cyberspace Academy.

Cyberspace Academy is a place for learning and playing, talking and seeing, inventing and interacting. Cyberspace Academy does not exist anywhere but in this book, yet it is the place where you will go to find out everything about the Internet that Kate and Zack did. So tighten your safety belts, you are going to take a trip with us back to the place and time when Kate and Zack first started learning about the Internet. Are you ready, Cadet? Let's go!

Kate and Zack stare at the message scrolling across their computer screen:

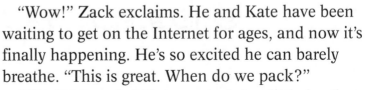

File	Edit	View

CONGRATULATIONS!

You have been accepted into Cyberspace Academy.

"Wow!" Zack exclaims. He and Kate have been waiting to get on the Internet for ages, and now it's finally happening. He's so excited he can barely breathe. "This is great. When do we pack?"

"We don't pack," Kate reminds her little brother. "This is the computer age. We don't have to actually take a bus or walk to Cyberspace Academy—it comes to us through the computer."

On the screen the message continues:

Your mission as Cyberspace Cadets is to graduate with enough training so you can pilot your computer safely through the Internet. Once on the Internet you will search out new and exciting information, play games, and travel all over the world—all while sitting at your computer! You will also meet new friends who are surfing the Net on similar missions.

"So when do we begin?" asks Zack, who can't wait to get started. Kate has to admit that she is pretty excited, too.

"You begin right now." The voice comes from inside their computer! There on the screen, Kate and Zack see a cool-looking young guy in a cyberspace uniform with sergeant's stripes on his collar. "I'm your guide through basic training, First Sergeant Abraham Lincoln Kennedy. But you can call me CyberSarge. So what are you kids waiting for? Let's get started on your first assignment!"

Both Kate and Zack are a bit nervous. It's one thing to read about the Internet in books and magazines, or to watch it on TV shows—but this is the real thing. They are about to plug in to the digital generation. They are on the verge of becoming real Internauts, today's equivalent of astronauts who travel in space, only Internauts travel online in *cyber*space.

"Don't sweat it, kids," says CyberSarge. "You may just be newbies now—but come graduation day, both of you will be navigating the Internet like pros."

"What's a newbie?" asks Kate.

"Good question!" responds CyberSarge. "There are a lot of new words you'll be hearing during your training. If you look down at the side screen of your computer, you'll see a window with a little bookworm perched on top. Whenever there's a new word—what I like to call *geek speak*—then the bookworm will tell you what that word means."

CyberSarge points over to the side of the screen where the bookworm explains the two new words he has just used.

"Being a geek sounds like fun," says Zack.

"It can be," agrees CyberSarge. "But geeks often

WHO IS CYBERSARGE?

CyberSarge, like Cyberspace Academy, exists only in this book. He is a helpful guy who has all the information Kate, Zack, and you need to learn about the Internet. While you won't find him anywhere else, if you pay attention to what he has to say in this book, you will soon be surfing the Internet like a pro!

GEEKS

Geeks are people who are really excited by computers and are proud of it.

GEEK SPEAK

Geek speak refers to words that are usually only used in reference to computers and being on the Internet.

CYBERSARGE SAYS:

We're all new here in cyberspace. When you become an expert, remember how you felt your first day online and treat other newbies the way you would have wanted to be treated.

NEWBIE

This is what everyone is called the first time they log on to the Internet. It just means someone who's learning their way around. There's nothing wrong with being a newbie—we are all newbies whenever we try to do something new.

spend too much time on their computers surfing the Net and playing games. They forget about doing their chores around the house and finishing their homework. They even ignore their friends."

"I'd never do that," promises Kate. "Now what's a newbie?"

"That's us," Zack admits. "We're new users. We're newbies."

"So what do we learn first?" asks Kate. She doesn't want to remain a newbie one minute longer than she has to.

"Well, the best place to start is to learn a little bit about where the Internet came from and what it is today." CyberSarge steps aside to let the kids' first lesson scroll across the computer screen:

File	Edit	View

A SHORT HISTORY OF THE INTERNET

Once upon a time, way back in 1969, people in colleges and governments were just learning how to use computers to solve problems. They used simple word processors to write down what they learned and store it in their computers, but there were no daily updated libraries where people could go to read what other people had just written and add to it.

So someone who worked for the government in an agency called the Defense Advanced Research Projects Agency came up with the idea that several computers could be linked together by telephone wires so they could "talk" to one another. A note that was written on one computer could be sent

immediately to all the other computers. So they wired four computers together in a group. They called that group of computers a **network**. The network's name was **DARPANET**, after the first letters in the name: **D**efense **A**dvanced **R**esearch **P**rojects **A**gency with **NET** (meaning **network** here) added to the end.

The network was a great idea and it quickly grew. The name was shortened by dropping the "D" and calling it simply **ARPANET**.

ARPANET grew and grew over time, adding more and more computers over phone wires. In 1983 the military research people thought they would be better off having their own private network so they created the **MILNET** network.

The idea of networks caught on, and in 1984 another government agency, the **N**ational **S**cience **F**oundation, started the **NSFNET** network, which linked together five supercomputer centers and made the information available to **any** school that needed it.

The way it worked was that everyone who entered a network was connected to at least one of the supercomputer centers. That supercomputer gave them access to all the other computers on the network—even to those places that were hooked into the network through another gateway.

Think of gateways as doors that let you go inside the house where a supercomputer lives. Once you're in the house, you can pick up the supercomputer's telephone and call anyone else who has a computer hooked up to a telephone. Like most really smart ideas, this networking idea was actually very simple.

The NSFNET became very popular. More computers and more wires had to be added because everyone in schools and government wanted to get onto the network. Instead of just adding more computers into the first

NETWORK

A network is simply a group of computers joined together so they can communicate with one another. A network can be as small as two computers joined together by phone lines in an office, or as large as millions of computers spread all over the world and joined by telephone lines, satellite relays, fiber optic cables, or radio links.

GATEWAY

A gateway is a computer system that acts as a translator between different types of computers to allow them to interact in cyberspace.

MAINFRAMES

These are large computers—sometimes taking up a whole room!—that are usually found in big companies and colleges and are used by many people. Mainframes are expensive and often need special air-conditioned rooms. While many mainframes are still being used, they are rapidly being replaced by smaller computers, even by personal desktop or laptop computers like yours.

SUPERCOMPUTER

This is a mainframe-sized computer that operates much faster than a normal desktop or laptop computer, and is used for special science and military projects.

network of supercomputers, they added more networks and wired all the networks together. They called all these interconnected networks an **Inter-Net-Network.**

Today we call it the **Internet**. And because lots of people now have their own personal computers, the Internet is even more popular. In the last 10 years it has grown from about 5,000 users to more than 30 million today—with thousands of new computer users coming online every month.

"Wow!" says Kate, amazed. "That's a lot of users."

"And a lot of wires," Zack adds.

"In the old days when your parents were kids, phone lines hooked up the networks together all over the country," CyberSarge says. "Now a lot of the hookups take place on new fiber optic cables that are much smaller and carry a lot more information a lot faster. Some computers are even hooked into satellites. Today the whole world is linked into the Internet."

ONLINE

Being online means that you are connected to another computer, usually through a modem, and your user name and password has been accepted by that remote computer. Often, this means the same thing as **logged on.**

OFFLINE

Offline means that you have left the remote computer and your modem has hung up. Often, this means the same thing as **logged off.**

MODEM

Modem stands for **modulator-demodulator**. It's a device that allows your computer to link up with other computers over telephone lines.

REMOTE COMPUTER

A remote computer is another computer connected to your computer through telephone lines (or through other network connections).

USER NAME

That's the name you use to log on to a network. Usually someone has given you permission to log on to the network and has recorded your user name in the network's databank. That way, everyone who wants to, can know when you are actively **on** the network.

"The whole world! Wow!" Kate's eyes light up as she imagines all the places she will be able to visit, all the new friends she will make. "This is going to be fun!"

"It will be," CyberSarge promises. "But before you two go leaping out into cyberspace on your own, you need some surfing lessons."

"We're ready!" Kate and Zack reply in unison.

PASSWORD

A password is a secret name that you and only you know. After you enter your user name, you are asked to enter your secret name. That way no one can get onto a network and pretend to be you.

FIBER OPTIC

Fiber optics are new, high-speed cables that are much smaller than the old wire cables used for telephone lines. They can carry much more information at much faster speeds. Most long-distance phone traffic is already carried in digital form, through high-volume fiber optic cables.

DIGITAL

Computers "talk" to other computers digitally. In other words, they store and process information as a series of numbers. Anything—including words, pictures, and sounds—can be "digitized" into the computer, then "undigitized" with a software program so you can read the words, hear the sounds, or see the pictures.

SOFTWARE PROGRAM

These are the instructions that tell the computer what you want it to do.

SURFING

Traveling through cyberspace through your computer is often called **surfing**.

Chapter 1

Life on the Internet:

What's It All About?

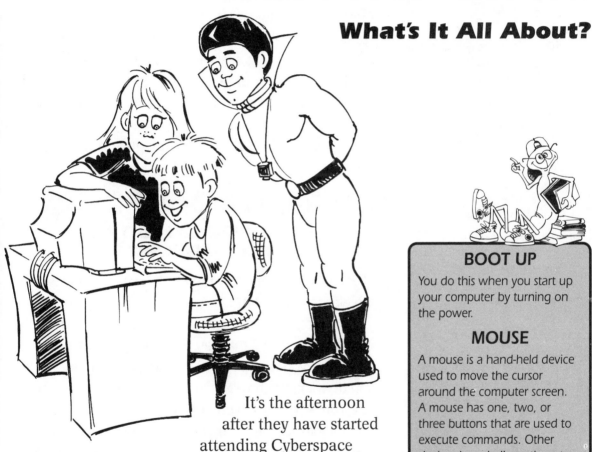

It's the afternoon after they have started attending Cyberspace Academy. Kate and Zack sit at their computer terminal anxious to get going again. Kate boots up their computer, and a few seconds later CyberSarge appears on the screen.

"Ready to blast off!" Zack exclaims enthusiastically.

CyberSarge smiles. He likes the fact that kids today are eager to learn to do so much with their

BOOT UP

You do this when you start up your computer by turning on the power.

MOUSE

A mouse is a hand-held device used to move the cursor around the computer screen. A mouse has one, two, or three buttons that are used to execute commands. Other devices have balls on them to move the cursor, and some newer ones have pads that trace the movement of your finger to move the cursor.

CURSOR

A cursor is a blinking box or line on your computer screen that indicates where the next character you type will go.

E-MAIL

E-mail is **electronic mail**, which just means that it is sent by the computer rather than through your local post office.

CHAT

An online chat is a lot like talking to someone on the phone, only you type out your words on your computer rather than speak out loud.

LOG ON

Log on is what you do when you connect to a remote computer. Usually you will be asked for a user name (the name the computer knows you by) and your password. If you don't have a user name on that computer you can often use **guest** or **visitor** as both your user name and password.

LOG OFF

Log off is what you do when you leave the remote computer. You usually log off by typing or clicking **bye**, **exit**, **goodbye**, or **quit**.

KEY PAL

Key pals are pen pals that you talk to through the computer. Since you use a keyboard to type your e-mail letters, pen pals in cyberspace are called **key pals**.

computers. "OK," he says. "Strap in and hang on tight. Next stop—cyberspace!"

Kate holds her mouse tightly in her hand. This is exciting. "What do I do?" she asks.

"Today, you two can just sit back and leave the driving to an old timer—namely me," says CyberSarge. "I'm going to take you on a short, guided tour on the Internet so you'll get the lay of the land. In the next sessions, we'll go through each part of the Internet in detail—but today you'll just sit back and watch to get a feel for what life can be like on the Internet."

The kids watch as their next lesson scrolls on the screen:

File	Edit	View

WHAT YOU CAN DO ON THE INTERNET

It's nice to know that the Internet is here, but why would we want to go visit it?

The simple answer is that the Internet—like your computer—is a tool that can help you grow smarter.

Think of your computer as a "brain machine" that helps you do things with your mind, the way a hammer and screwdriver can help you build things with your hands.

Now think of the Internet as "brain food" that lets you imagine more things and do more things with your mind.

People say we live in an "Information Society" where "the more you know, the more you grow." CyberSarge thinks this is true.

The Internet can help you grow smarter in five very basic ways:

1. COMMUNICATING

With e-mail and chat groups you will be able to talk to kids and grownups all over the world. You might find a key pal in Paris or talk to a scientist at the South Pole. By talking and listening you are communicating with people from different places with different ways of looking at life. On the Internet your neighborhood is the whole wide world!

2. EXPLORING

The Internet connects you to the rest of the world and lets you explore places and ideas online. You can become a virtual tourist, visiting other cities and countries through your computer. You can actually tour through the famous museums in Europe, or even go on a voyage to the planets and moons in our solar system. Wherever you want to go, there you are—on the Internet.

3. FINDING

Everything is connected to everything else on the Internet. So start anywhere, and you can find just about anything you want to find. It might be the definition to a word, or some historical facts for your homework assignment. Whatever it is you are looking for, chances are you can find it somewhere on the Internet. When you become full-fledged Internauts you'll know how to conduct searches to find what you're looking for.

VIRTUAL TOURIST

Being a virtual tourist simply means visiting places in cyberspace without having to physically go there. You go there online and in your imagination.

INTERNAUTS

These are astronauts who are exploring the new frontiers of cyberspace rather than outer space.

4. LEARNING

There are two ways you'll learn while surfing the Net. One way is when you go searching for something you want to know about, like who invented the bicycle. The other way is something called "serendipity," which means finding something new and unexpected by accident. Serendipitous learning—or learning through serendipity—happens all the time on the Internet. And it is fun!

5. PLAYING

All work and no play makes for dull boys and girls. That's really true. Having fun and playing games can stretch your imagination. It opens up new ways of looking at the world. And there are lots of ways to play on the Internet.

"Let's take a closer look at each one of these ways to learn and grow on the Internet," CyberSarge says as he pops up on the computer screen. "We'll start with *communicating*."

"I know e-mail is sending letters and chatting is communicating—like on the telephone—only you talk with your keyboard rather than your mouth," says Kate.

"I have a deaf friend," Zack adds. "Sometimes he writes things down on a notepad so I'll understand."

"That's one of the nice things about the Internet," says CyberSarge. "It doesn't matter who you are or what you look like. You can be anyone or anything and it's fine because people will only know you by what you type in."

"I like that," Kate says in a matter-of-fact tone. "You can really make friends and get to know someone—without worrying about how you look or the clothes you wear."

"That's the good news about the Internet," says CyberSarge.

"So what's the bad news?" wonders Zack.

"The bad news about the Internet is that some people take advantage of it. They hide themselves in disguises—like wearing a Halloween costume—and you're not always sure who they really are."

"So what do we do about that?" asks Kate.

"The same thing you do when you answer the telephone and you're not sure who you're talking to," replies CyberSarge. "Don't answer personal questions about yourself, your parents, or your home. The Internet is kind of like the old telephone system."

"How's that?" Zack asks.

"In the old days there were party lines, which meant that you could call up one phone number that a lot of other people were already talking on, and all those other people could hear what you were saying on the phone. It's that way on the Internet. Other people might be listening in. The rule to remember is: *Don't say anything on the Internet that you wouldn't feel right saying out loud in public.*"

"We'll definitely remember that rule," Kate promises.

"Good!" says CyberSarge with a smile. "Now let's look at how we *communicate* on the Internet."

CYBERSARGE SAYS:

When you are on the Internet, you should never answer personal questions about yourself such as what your real name is; what your actual home address is; where your school is located; or even your parents' full names, their job titles, or where they work. For more guidelines, refer to Chapter 5: The Top Ten Rules for Surfing the Net, starting on page 101, and Chapter 10: Parents' Guide, starting on page 167.

SNAIL MAIL

Snail mail is the paper mail that comes through a slot in your front door or is deposited in a box mounted outside your house or apartment. It's called that by Internauts because it's so much slower than e-mail.

COMMUNICATING

There are three basic ways to communicate on the Internet. Two of the basic ways of communicating are personal (e-mail, chatting and group chatting). The third basic way is general (mailing lists and newsgroups). We'll take them one at a time.

The first way we communicate personally is through e-mail. That's by writing a letter, sending it to someone, and then getting a reply. People used to write letters on paper to one another all the time. We don't do that as much anymore because we have the telephone. But now with the Internet we're learning how to write letters again.

E-mail works just like snail mail—which is what Internauts call the regular mail the post office delivers to your house. The big difference is that e-mail is delivered in cyberspace.

The second way to communicate personally is by chatting. You call up someone through the Internet and "talk" to them the way you do on the phone, only you're writing and reading on your computer rather than talking and listening with a phone in your hand.

Sometimes you're chatting with just one person, but there are also "chat groups" where many people can be talking at the same time. Chat groups can be a little confusing because several people may try to talk at one time. But there are rules for chatting that we'll discuss later in the book to help you out.

The third way of communicating is general. It is a bit like group chatting, because there is more than one other person you're communicating with, but now you're communicating through mailing lists and newsgroups.

LISTSERVER

A listserver is a program that automatically sends and receives e-mail to and from a particular group of subscribers.

SERVER

A server is a computer attached to a network. A server can distribute information or files automatically in response to specifically worded e-mail requests. Think of a server like a receptionist in an office; the receptionist knows where to direct all the calls that come in.

CHAT GROUPS

Chat groups are online addresses where many people talk to each other at once.

MAILING LISTS

Mailing lists are simply lists of Internet users who subscribe to the list just like they would subscribe to a magazine. When you send an e-mail letter to a mailing list, everyone on the list gets a copy. If you subscribe to the list, you get copies of every letter written to the list, too.

HEADERS

These are phrases at the start of a message that tell you what the message is about. They are like headlines in a newspaper that tell you what a particular news story is about.

There are mailing lists that you can subscribe to just as you would subscribe to a favorite magazine. Some of these lists have hundreds of people subscribing. When you write a letter to such a group everyone on the list gets a copy of your letter. And you get a copy in your e-mail mailbox of every letter written to the list, too.

Mailing lists are usually handled by a Listserver, a special program that automatically sorts the incoming messages and then sends them out to all the current list subscribers. That can be a lot of letters, so be careful about how many lists you subscribe to—or you may end up with a hundred letters every day, and the more time you spend online reading, the more it will cost you.

When mailing lists get really popular, they often become Usenet newsgroups. With newsgroups you subscribe to the group, but instead of hundreds of e-mail letters, you get a list of headers from the articles that have been posted since the last time you checked. This way you can choose to read only those articles that interest you. You can also follow a particular thread without having to read all the other articles. Think of newsgroups as bulletin boards where people are tacking up new notes and replying to old ones.

USENET NEWSGROUPS

Usenet newsgroups are online groups in which you can discuss almost any subject you can imagine—from how to house-train your pet to what the latest UFO rumor is. There are currently over 10,000 active Internet newsgroups.

ARTICLES

Letters that are posted in newsgroups are often referred to as articles rather than letters. This is because when you use mailing lists you are usually answering one person—even though everyone on the mailing list can read your letter. But in newsgroups you are often writing comments to the whole group, much like a reporter writing an article for everyone who subscribes to a particular magazine.

THREADS

Threads are discussions within a newsgroup—or mailing list—on a certain topic. Threads are identified by the message header. For instance, if you have subscribed to a newsgroup about pets, you may only want to read and reply to the threads about cats.

"E-mail sounds great!" Kate exclaims. She is thinking about all the key pals she could write to, such as her friend Julie who moved to Florida, and whom she knows has a computer.

"E-mail is the most popular way to use the Internet," answers CyberSarge with a nod.

"What if I don't write so well?" asks Zack, who can only remember writing two letters in his whole life.

"It's something you'll learn quickly," replies CyberSarge. "Because we do so much talking on the telephone, we've forgotten how to write down our thoughts. That's a good thing about the Internet and e-mail: It forces us to think about what we're going to say and to say it simply. Short and sweet is the rule for e-mail."

"Sometimes it's hard to say what you mean by just using words," says Kate. She often uses a lot of facial expressions and hand gestures to punctuate her words when she gets into a really serious discussion.

"That's what smileys are for," says CyberSarge.

"What's a smiley?" ask Kate and Zack together.

CyberSarge smiles and points to the computer screen where the kids see:

SMILEYS AND ACRONYMS

When you're face-to-face, you can smile, frown, and make all kinds of facial expressions to enhance your words. You can also sound happy, sad, angry, or just plain bored. In e-mail, your words have to carry your thoughts by themselves—so folks invented **smileys** to punctuate their phrases.

There are two types of basic smileys: those with pictures and those with words.

The picture smileys are made up of different combinations of punctuation marks. Look at them sideways to get the idea. They include:

:-)	smile with a nose
:)	smile without a nose
:*)	just clowning around
:-D	said with a smile
:-!	you put your foot in your mouth
:-,	said with a smirk
:/)	it's not funny
:-"	pursing your lips
(:-&	you're angry
:-o	you're shouting or I'm shocked
:-@	you're SCREAMING
:-(	you're unhappy
:-c	you're really unhappy
:,-(	you're crying
(:-(	you're sad
||*(	offering a handshake
||*)	accepting a handshake
||	giving a hug
:-x	giving a kiss
:-J	said with tongue in cheek
:-P	no way!
:-b	sticking my tongue out

@>—>—	offering a rose
:-X	not saying a word
:-*	oops!
`-)	said with a wink
:-C	that's unbelievable!
:@	what?
<:-)	dunce
<{:-)}	message in a bottle
:>)	big nose
&:-)	curly hair
#:-)	matted hair
8-)	wearing glasses
d:-o	hats off to a great idea
:-I	playing a harmonica
O:-)	what an angel
(-:	left-handed
=:-)	punk rocker
:-*	after eating something bitter
:-6	after eating something sour

There are word smileys that indicate emotions. They are called **emoticons** (short for "emotion" and "icon"), and they are inserted into text between brackets < >. Some emoticons are:

        <amazed>
        <angrily>
        <applauding>
        <blush>
        <chuckle>
        <crying>
        <frown>
        <grin> or just plain <g>
        <laughing>
        <silly grin>
        <smile>
        <smirk>
        <wink>

<blush>

Other smileys with words are called **acronyms**. Acronyms are just shortcuts that are used in e-mail. It's like saying "OK" instead of "okay," or "BTW" to mean "by the way." Some common acronyms are:

ADN	any day now
AFKBRB	away from keyboard be right back
ASAP	as soon as possible
B4N	bye for now
BAD	broken as designed
BBS	bulletin board system
BL	belly laugh(ing)
BMN	but maybe not
BRB	be right back
BTA	but then again
BTW	by the way
CU	see you
CUL	see you later
DTRT	do the right thing
F2F	face to face
FAQ	frequently asked question
FITB	fill in the blank
FWIW	for what it's worth
FYI	for your information
GAL	get a life
GIGO	garbage in, garbage out (which means what comes out is as only as good as what's put in)
GIWIST	gee, I wish I'd said that
GMTA	great minds think alike
HELP	helping energetic little people
IAE	in any event
IC	I see
ILY	I love you
IRL	in real life
IMCO	in my considered opinion
IME	in my experience
IMHO	in my humble opinion

CYBERSARGE SAYS:

On the Web, you can travel to Internet sites all over the world. But don't worry, even in other countries where English is not the dominant language, the primary language of the Web is English. So while you might visit a site in Spain, chances are the language used will be English, even though there may be special pages or hyperlinks that can guide you to a section where the information can also be found in Spanish.

LOL

IMO	in my opinion
INPO	in no particular order
IOW	in other words
JIC	just in case
JTYWTK	just thought you wanted to know
KMYF	kiss me you fool
KWIM	know what I mean?
LJBF	let's just be friends
LOL	laughing out loud
LTNS	long time no see
NBIF	no basis in fact
OHDH	old habits die hard
OTOH	on the other hand
PMBI	pardon my butting in
POV	point of view
PTB	powers that be
ROTFL	rolling on the floor laughing
RPG	role-playing games
RSVP	répondez s'il vous plaît (French for **please reply**)
SFLA	stupid four-letter acronym
SIG	special interest group
SYSOP	the SYStem OPerator
TGIF	thank God it's Friday
TIA	thanks in advance
TLA	three-letter acronym
TTBOMK	to the best of my knowledge
WFM	works for me
WYSIWYG	what you see is what you get

"Cool!" exclaims Zack. "I can even make up my own acronyms—like WTFS: watch that first step."

"That's right," CyberSarge confirmed. "And when you invent an acronym, you just type it out in capital letters, then you type what it means. Who knows, people might just like it enough to start using it!"

"Cool!" comments Kate. "Now what do we do next?"

"The next major reason for being on the Internet is to be an *explorer*," says CyberSarge.

"That's me!" says Zack. "I love to explore and go where no kid has gone before."

"Traveling on the Internet is like discovering a new galaxy. You'll find all kinds of new places to visit, learn new things, meet new friends. And because there are new places coming online every day, you'll never be able to visit all of them."

"How many places are there?" asks Kate.

"By the end of 1995 there will be more than 50,000 home pages on the World Wide Web."

"Home pages?" asks Kate, a puzzled look on her face.

"World Wide Web?" asks Zack, frowning. CyberSarge explains.

| File | Edit | View |

WORLD WIDE WEB

The World Wide Web—which is also called **the WWW**, or just **the Web**—is not the only service available on the Internet, but it's rapidly becoming one of the most popular. It's got pictures and hypertext—which means you can jump from one place to another, all over the world, with a single click of a mouse or a few keys typed on a keyboard.

The Web was started in Switzerland by CERN, the European Laboratory for Particle Physics. The people at CERN wanted to build a hypermedia system with hyperlinks to other systems so it would be easier to use the Internet.

The advantage of using hypertext is that in a hypertext document, if you want more information about the particular subject, you can usually just click on it with your mouse to read further details. If you don't know what the word means, you can click on it and a definition will pop up.

Documents can also be (and often are) linked to other documents by completely different authors—much like the footnotes in your textbooks at school. But instead of having to turn to another chapter or even get another book, with hypertext links you can get the referenced document instantly.

To access the Web, you need to run a Web browser program. The Web browser reads documents and can display pictures. And, when you click on a hypertext link, it can fetch documents from other sources on the Internet.

Web browsers can also access files by a range of methods including FTP, NNTP, and Gopher™, all of which we will discuss later.

Some servers have search capabilities, which means you can locate documents and databases by searching for specific words and phrases.

"OK," says Kate. "I'm beginning to understand the Web. But what's a home page?"

"The World Wide Web is like a building," says CyberSarge. "Think of a home page as an office in that building. The office can have many rooms or just one room. That means that a home page can contain other pages or other documents all grouped together."

"What do you mean by other pages?" asked Zack.

"Well, look at it this way," explains CyberSarge. "Home pages on the Web are often set up by individual people or companies who want to do business on the Internet. For instance, MCA/Universal, a huge company, set up a Web site, or home page, where they could advertise their movies and TV shows. Other smaller companies owned by MCA/Universal, including the publishers of this book, want to advertise their books, too. So the publishing company adds pages to MCA/Universal's home page."

"So when you click on MCA/Universal's home page, you can see a list of books as well as movies?" asks Kate.

"Correct!" says CyberSarge with a smile. "You click on highlighted words and icons in MCA/Universal's home page and those words and icons will lead you to other pages. Other Web sites might only have a single home page."

"The Web sounds like a really great place for exploring," says Zack.

"It is," agrees CyberSarge. "It's also becoming one of the best ways for *finding* something on the Internet."

"The Internet is so big," Kate says. "It's kind of like panning for gold. How do you find the nuggets in all that information?"

"It can be confusing. Think of the Internet as a school library, with books organized by subject or author name." CyberSarge frowns, then continues. "Actually, now that I think about it, the Internet is more like a book warehouse than a library, because the books on the Internet aren't always labeled as clearly or organized as well as they are in a library."

"I need to know about Thomas Jefferson for my homework assignment," Kate remarks. "Where would I start looking?"

CYBERSARGE SAYS:

Some home pages have text-only versions so you don't have to spend a lot of time downloading pictures. It's not always as pretty, but it's a lot faster.

NNTP

NNTP stands for Network News Transfer Protocol. These are local servers which distribute Usenet newsgroups throughout the globe.

GOPHER™

Gopher™ is a very popular Internet service on the Web that lets you look through all kinds of online text libraries for information.

"We'll take a closer look at some of the search engines you can use later on in this book. But for now let's take a quick look at two basic ways you can search the Internet," answers CyberSarge.

File	Edit	View

FINDING IT ON THE INTERNET

The Internet contains thousands of places and millions of documents. Finding what you want can be difficult, and can take a very long time if you don't narrow down your search.

One way to start is to go to the places that are most likely to contain the information you're looking for. You can start at a home page like Yahoo, which contains a list to date of almost 40,000 Web sites. Remember that a Web site is a computer location, much like a building. Inside the building are rooms like home pages, and inside the home pages are additional pages.

Fortunately Web sites are broken down by subjects so that you can find those that deal with Astronomy or Medicine, or whatever topic you're looking for.

Once you find the site with the subject you are looking for, you can go to other sites covering the same subject through hyperlinks.

The other way to look for places and documents on the Internet is to use a search engine or a program called Gopher™ to look for key words.

To find something on the Internet, the most important thing is to know just what you're looking for and to select the key words that will get you there. We'll do some sample searches later on to show you some tricks in finding things on the Internet.

SEARCH CAPABILITIES

This just means that there is an index that can be searched. Think of this like the card files in your local library. You can search through them to see if there are books in the library on the subject you are interested in.

DATABASES

Think of these as electronic file cabinets containing data—or information—that is somehow related. For example, a hospital's database might contain information on all the patients in that hospital, and a school's database would contain information on all the students attending that school.

ICON

An icon is a small image on the computer screen that you point at and click on with your mouse pointer to get to another program or to use a function within that program. Usually icons are pictures that represent the program or type of function in the software. For instance, if you click on the icon on your screen that represents your hard drive, you will open up the hard drive and be able to see which files and documents are inside it.

"Exploring and finding are all about *learning*," concludes CyberSarge.

"It sounds like too much fun to be learning," Zack says with a smile.

CyberSarge returns the smile. "Learning is *supposed* to be fun. Think about the things you know most about."

"Softball and astronomy are my best subjects," says Kate without hesitation.

"That's because you enjoy reading and doing them. The really good thing about the Internet is that it can make things that you're *not* excited about much more interesting. You'll be learning new things all the time on the Internet," explains CyberSarge.

"OK. We've covered communicating, exploring, finding, and learning. That leaves playing," Zack says eagerly.

"The Internet is full of games," says CyberSarge. "One of the most popular types of games is called a MUD."

File	Edit	View

PLAYING MUDS

MUDs are online, imaginary worlds that are built from words and look like parts of stories. These **virtual worlds**, as they are sometimes called, are the latest rage on campuses all around the world. MUDS—or Multiple User Dimensions—are electronic games and adventures which run on a large network, usually fueled by university computers. Players will often spend hours logged on to fantasy worlds based on science fiction stories or popular novels about dragons and wizards.

MUDs are like the hundreds of text-based, adventure video games that have gotten really popular with people who have access to their own computers. Since the

SEARCH ENGINE

Search engines are programs that are designed to go out into the Internet and search for the information you requested. Think of them as librarians who give you a list of possible books to read to find out what you want to know, then they go help you find the books.

KEY WORDS

Most documents contain specific or **key** words that tell you a bit about what the document is about. For example, the key words **baseball**, **pitcher**, and **World Series** would tell you that the document is about World Series baseball pitchers. Often, if you do a search just by titles of documents, you might not find what you are looking for. But using key words will get you inside the document where the information you are looking for might be hidden.

original MUD was created, several hundred MUD games have cropped up around the world.

There are newer MUDs coming online that use images as well as words to create virtual-reality–like worlds on the Internet.

"I can't wait to play in a MUD," Zack says with enthusiasm.

"They can be fun," CyberSarge agrees. "But like anything you enjoy, you have to be careful not to overdo it. Right now it's time to quit for the day. Tomorrow I'll show you how to go online for real."

VIRTUAL REALITY

Virtual reality, or VR, is a world that exists only at a specific VR arcade or in cyberspace. To experience today's virtual reality at a specific VR arcade, you physically walk to the arcade and suit up in a special helmet or glasses, gloves, and a body suit. These items are connected to VR devices through a computer in the arcade. When you walk, move, speak, smell, hear, or touch something, it seems to you as if you are **actually in** an imaginary world.

To experience today's virtual reality in cyberspace, you put on glasses—maybe also using gloves or your mouse at home—then you log on to a VR site in cyberspace. Once online you can walk around three-dimensional objects, move things, and communicate with other users through your keyboard. Some cyberspace VR sites also may be voice-activated soon, meaning you will be able to speak into your home computer's microphone to enter commands.

Chapter 2

Preparing for Liftoff:

How Do I Get Online?

When Kate and Zack turn on their computer and sit down in front of the screen the next afternoon, CyberSarge is waiting for them. This is the big day. Today they are plugging in to the Internet for real.

"I have one question before we start," says Kate.

"Ask away," replies CyberSarge.

"Well, we have a PC computer with Windows™. But my friend, Lisa, has a Macintosh™. Can we both plug in to the Internet?"

"No problem. There is software for both personal computers (PCs) and Macintosh systems. Almost all the commercial online services—such as America Online, CompuServe, and Prodigy—support both types of computers. So do the popular Internet software programs such as Netscape™ which is used

CYBERSARGE SAYS:

When you're online and need help, you can **usually get it by simply typing in the word** help**. Sometimes you can type in a** ? **and get help. Most computer systems and software programs will have a help menu or help key that you can use to get assistance. Whenever you start up a new program or log on to a remote computer, make a note of how you can get help if you need it.**

UNIX™

UNIX™ is a computer language that was developed by AT&T and is used on many educational computers. Many computer sites on the Internet run under the UNIX™ operating system.

COMPUTER LANGUAGE

A computer language is a system that allows different types of computers to speak to each other. Basically, computers translate English (or any other human language) into numbers because every computer can understand numbers.

DOWNLOADING

When you download you are recieving information to your computer from another computer, usually through a modem.

BBS

Bulletin Board Systems (BBS) are networks that your computer can dial into through your modem.
You communicate with other people by exchanging messages and files. You can also take pictures and information and download these to your own computer.

GRAPHICS

Graphics are images and pictures.

for browsing the World Wide Web, and Eudora™ which is used for e-mail."

"What're we waiting for?" prompts Zack, anxious to get started.

"Well, the first thing is to get a gateway into the Internet," says CyberSarge.

"What's a gateway again?" Kate looks puzzled.

"Remember how all the computers on the Internet are connected to one another?" CyberSarge asks. "Well, we need to connect up to one of those computers. That computer system we connect to is known as our Internet gateway server."

CyberSarge steps aside so the kids can read the lesson on the screen:

File	Edit	View

INTERNET GATEWAY SERVERS

There are four basic ways for you to access the Internet through your personal computer or Macintosh™:

1. SHELL ACCOUNT ACCESS

This is the simplest way to go online. It's almost like logging on to a local computer bulletin board system, which is called a BBS. You can send e-mail messages and download files. Most shell accounts have very little or no graphics, and often they require you to learn UNIX™ commands to operate them. Shell accounts usually aren't very pretty, but they are cheap. Currently, you can sign on to a local shell account computer for as little as $10 a month.

2. COMMERCIAL SERVICE ACCESS

The most popular commercial online services—America Online, CompuServe, Delphi, eWorld, and Prodigy—all have gateways into the Internet. Any of these services can be a good way to start surfing the Net since they have simple icons that make it easy to get help when you're online.

You also have access to their other services as well, including e-mail, which they will provide you the software for.

Until recently you really couldn't get to the Internet from these services but now most of the commercial services have full-featured Internet programs so you can go almost anywhere you want to on the Net.

The downside of commercial services is that you are usually limited to using their software, so even if you have a great e-mail program that isn't part of your online service, you won't be able to use it. The cost of using both the basic commercial services and accessing the Internet through the commercial services can also be very expensive if you're online a lot.

3. SLIP/PPP DIAL-UP ACCESS

SLIP (**S**erial **L**ine **I**nterface **P**rotocol) and **PPP** (**P**oint-to-**P**oint **P**rotocol) are a step up from a shell account. Here you are connected directly to the Internet through a service provider who has a computer gateway into the Internet and will let you use it for a price.

Currently there are national providers—such as Netcruiser™ and Pipeline™—that give you the basic Internet services through their own software for about $20 a month. There are also national and local providers that give you a software package or let you use your own. There's a wide range of cost, but full access to the Net with unlimited time is normally between $25 and $40 a month.

The good news about Netcruiser™ or Pipeline™ is they are simple to install and give you one menu of options to select from. The bad news is they are not as powerful as programs like Netscape™ or Eudora™.

CYBERSARGE SAYS:

Setting up a SLIP/PPP account with a local provider is not always easy. Take it one step at a time. Your local provider will usually have software that is already set up for their system to make it easier to get online.

INSTALL
This means setting up a software program so that it runs on your computer.

INSTALLATION PROGRAM
This is a program that often comes with software to install it onto your computer. Sometimes this is called a **setup program**.

SET UP
This means installing a software program onto your computer.

CYBERSARGE SAYS:

There are several Internet software packages at your local computer store. These are usually not that expensive and most of them have automated installation programs that can connect you to a national service provider. If you want to use one of these service providers this can be a quick and easy way to get online.

The real drawback to SLIP/PPP services is that you have to have TCP/IP software on your computer **before** you can connect.

4. LEASED-LINE ACCESS

This is really the same as a SLIP/PPP account except that you are using a high-speed direct line instead of a regular phone line to go online. It's much faster, but also much more expensive. However, ISDN—Integrated Services Digital Network—lines are being installed by the phone companies and will, in a short time, be available to your home or school currently for about $30 a month. This is in addition to your service provider costs. But the speed of traveling the Internet—which can be five to ten times faster with leased-line access than with a regular modem—may make it worthwhile if you have a lot of surfing to do.

For the rest of this lesson we're going to concentrate on the SLIP/PPP access. Even if you decide to use a commercial online service as your provider, the Internet software programs you will use will be about the same.

CyberSarge steps back into the center of their computer screen. "Once you've selected your online service provider, they will give you the information you need to connect to the Internet."

Kate and Zack tell CyberSarge that they need to continue the lesson later. Before they can go any further, they need to do some research about online services. [Refer to Chapter 8: Finding your Cybership, starting on page 151.] Then they need to talk to their parents.

Most online service accounts need to be held by an adult. They often require a credit card so they can automatically charge your monthly fee and your time online. Children can get their own e-mail addresses under the adult's account, but adults need to be included in this process.

Once Kate and Zack figure out which online service and account would work best for their needs, they talk to their parents about budgets and how much time the kids are allowed online every month. (If you are trying to get your school hooked up to the Internet, you would have this conversation with your teacher or your principal.) Their parents may have different ideas about what service is the best for the whole family, especially if they choose to use the Internet as well.

CYBERSARGE SAYS:

Right about now would be a perfect time to take this book to your parents or your teacher and have them read Chapter 10, which is a grown-ups' guide to their children's involvement in cyberspace. Chapter 10 starts on page167.

CYBERSARGE SAYS:

Here would be a good time to distinguish between
three different terms: service providers, Internet software, and online services.

Service providers are the companies that are set up to get you on the Internet; each service provider offers access to a different combination of things to do on the Internet.

Internet software is the software that your service provider sends you to get you onto the Internet through their company; there is a lot of different software, such as e-mail software, browsing software, and more.

Online services are the places and things available to you once you're on the Internet such as sites, databases, games, information, and more.

The family sits down and discusses all the options and reaches an agreement about the time the kids are allotted every month. That way their parents know what will be charged every month to their credit card. (No one likes unexpected or expensive surprises, parents least of all!) And since time online means that the telephone line will be tied up, their parents give them a specific schedule about which hours during the day they can go online.

Their parents also set limits for their kids about appropriate places for them to visit online; Kate and Zack agree not to visit Internet sites that have adult content such as pornography, which is definitely ***not***

OK for children. Then Kate and Zack's parents set up a series of chores for their kids to do around the house to "pay" for their time online. Everybody is happy with the agreement. Kate and Zack have learned already that being on the Internet may be fun, but that they have responsibilities as surfers as well.

Their parents telephone the agreed-upon service provider and set up an account. The service provider promises to send out the necessary software and a start-up manual to their home within a few days or a week. When all the information arrives, their parents hand them the package and Kate and Zack rush over to their computer.

Now they are ready to continue with their lesson!

"OK," says Kate. "We've selected a service provider in our city called MyNet. What do we do now?"

MYNET

MyNet is the made up name of the service provider that Kate and Zack choose. It is only a sample name in this book to help you learn about the Internet. When you are ready to go online, you will choose a **real** service provider. See Chapter 8: Finding Your Cybership, starting on page 151.

DISK DRIVE

This is the part inside the computer that transfers the information on your floppy disk into the computer's memory, or transfers what is in the computer's memory onto your hard disk. Think of this like a tape recorder that can play what is on the tape or can record music or words and put them on the tape. Disk drives come in two formats: a **hard drive** and a **floppy drive**.

HARD DISK

This is a magnetic disk that stores information and is permanently installed in your computer. Hard disks can hold much more information than floppy disks. They are also sometimes called **fixed disks**.

HARD DRIVE

This is a disk drive that reads and writes from hard disks.

LOG ON VERSUS LOG IN

These two terms mean the same thing.

CYBERSARGE SAYS:

When telling someone something that contains periods, like your e-mail address, you should use the word "dot" instead of saying "period." To say Kate's address, **kate@mynet.com,** *say:* **"kate at mynet dot com."**

TCP/IP

Transmission Control Protocol/Internet Protocol is a language converter that allows different computers on the Net to speak the same language. TCP/IP tells each computer how to send and receive packets of data, that often have to travel through multiple networks in order to reach their destinations. TCP/IP also checks that the information gets delivered in one piece, without errors.

CyberSarge speaks to them from the screen. "Install your software and get it running," he says. "I'll be here to help you if you need me."

Kate reads the list of files on the floppy disk label. "This looks complicated," she says. "There are so many different programs: e-mail, FTP, Telnet. . . ."

"Later on we'll discuss all those programs, one at a time," says Sarge. "For now, the first thing to do—and the hardest—is to get your computer connected to the Internet."

Their local Internet access provider has given the disk to them. Zack and Kate could also have gone to their local software store and bought commercial programs that would provide the same services.

Kate puts the floppy disk in the disk drive and types in: **A:INSTALL**.

In response, the Install program copies several programs to their computer's hard drive. The first is the TCP/IP program that allows their computer to contact their Internet service provider.

Zack reads instructions that their Internet provider has given them along with the floppy disk. "Whoa!" he says. "This looks like a math quiz!"

CyberSarge appears on the screen again. "This is the hardest part," he agrees. "But once you get up and running, you won't have to change anything here again." Kate scans the instructions. They have to set up, or configure, their TCP/IP program so that it knows how to talk to the Internet computer. The information they need to enter will be different from yours, but this is a sample of what their setup looks like. Kate decides to go first. The information Kate needs to enter is given to them on a sheet of paper, or in the manual, by the provider. She simply fills in the blanks:

File	Edit	View

IP Address:	1.1.1.1
Subnet Mask:	255.0.0.0
Host Name:	mynet.com
Domain Name:	mynet.com
Port:	com
Modem speed:	14,400
Dial:	(310) 555-0000
Log on:	[your log on name]
Password:	[Kate's private log on password]
Interface Name:	MyNet
Mail server name:	mail.mynet.com
Mail password:	[Kate's private log on password]
News server:	news.mynet.com
Domain servers:	222.222.68.160
	333.228.140.0
	444.228.8.7
Gateway address:	999.10.160.1

CYBERSARGE SAYS:

If she had a Macintosh™, Kate would click on the shaded or circled area around the word, Install. *In many instances in this book where a PC user will type in instructions, a Macintosh™ user will be instructed to use her or his mouse to click on boxes. Different installation software programs are usually pretty clear about what steps to take and when. So don't worry if your computer is not a PC, the instructions here will basically correspond to the specific instructions given by your installation software. Either way, be patient; this is the toughest part of surfing the Net. Once you get your Internet software set up and installed, you've accomplished the hardest part!*

"Kate's setup form is only an example," says CyberSarge. "Your own setup program will be different, but this is the basic information that your service provider will give you in order to use their gateway to the Internet."

When Kate types in her private password for the last time, she lets Zack take over for the practice. He carefully studies the instructions as he fills in the blanks on the form on the computer screen.

"You're almost there," says CyberSarge from his place on the edge of the screen. He's watching to make sure Kate and Zack get it right. "Another tough part is copying down the numbers for domain servers."

"What are domain servers?" asks Zack.

"They're the addresses of the computers you'll be

FLOPPY DISK

This is a flexible, plastic-covered disk (usually 3.5 or 5.25 inches in size) that is inserted into a computer's floppy disk drive and used to transfer or store information. These are also called **diskettes**.

FLOPPY DRIVE

This is a disk drive that reads and writes from floppy disks. You stick a floppy disk into this drive.

ADDRESS

An Internet address is just like your home or apartment address, only it is in cyberspace. Once you have an Internet address, you have a place all your own on the Internet. All the Internet addresses given in this book are in **bold italics** to make sure the punctuation in them is not confused with regular punctuation. You do not need to use **bold** or *italics* when typing in any Internet addresses.

HOST

This is a computer that is connected directly to the Internet. Like a restaurant host who invites you into a restaurant and often seats you, a host computer acts as your gateway onto the Net.

talking to," answers CyberSarge. "Every server in the world has its own special address that is identified by these four groups of numbers, separated by periods."

Zack fills in the rest of the blanks, being very careful to copy the numbers from the instructions exactly as they are written.

"Cool!" Kate exclaims when Zack finishes. "Let's blast off!"

Zack and Kate both grab for the mouse. Kate wins. She clicks on the word *Connect* and their modem automatically dials the number of their service provider. They both watch anxiously for a moment—then the computer beeps as it makes contact.

"Congratulations, Cadets," CyberSarge tells them proudly. "You're now on the Internet! But before we do any real surfing on the Net, you'll need to know more about Internet addresses. We'll cover that in the next section."

Chapter 3

Pilot's Manual for the Internet:

What Do I Do Once I Get Online?

This is the big moment. Right now Kate and Zack are going to take their first cruise on the Internet. They have selected a local service provider, MyNet, as their Internet gateway. Both of them have their own address on the Internet. Kate's is **kate@mynet.com** and Zack's is **zack@mynet.com**.

They have learned that every Internet address has three parts:

1. The user name (like Kate or Zack, or even something strange like UU2020).

2. The @ sign, which means "at."

3. The address of the user's mail server.

Kate's user name is **kate** and on the Internet she is known as **kate@**—or kate "at"—**mynet.com**, which looks like: **kate@mynet.com**

If there had already been a **kate** on MyNet, she would have had to choose another user name, like **kat** or **kate2**.

The **mynet.com** part of the address is actually called a "domain" name. The domain name is based on an IP—or Internet Protocol—system. This system is simply a numerical and letter-based system that allows every server on the Internet to have a unique address that cannot be copied or used by any other server or user on the Net. IP addresses have been established so that every server on the Internet has its own unique address. Some domain names can be as long as ten characters. If Kate and Zack shared an address, it could be ***kateandzac@mynet.com***.

Addresses are usually read from left to right. Everything to the right of the @ sign is the domain. The word on the left of the @ sign is the user name. Sometimes domain names can be very long—like ***one.two.univ.edu***—but each letter and number to the right of the @ is all part of the domain name.

All IP addresses have four sets of numbers separated with periods, such as: ***999.200.8.100***. These numbers mean the same thing as something like ***mynet.com***—but where people find it easier to remember a name they can say and spell, computers are more comfortable with numbers.

Well, it's pretty easy to figure out what the ***mynet*** part of the domain name is. But what about the ***com*** part? CyberSarge has suggested the best way to read a domain name address is to start at the right and read backward.

The ***com*** part of the address tells you that the domain of ***kate@mynet.com*** is a *commercial* Internet site. Common domain abbreviations include:

- *edu* for educational sites, such as colleges
- ***com*** for commercial sites, such as commercial Internet service providers and big companies like MCA/Universal

DOMAIN NAME

This is the name given to a host computer on the Internet. The host computer is the one that is connected directly to the Internet.

gov for government sites, such as the White House or the Library of Congress

mil for military sites, such as the Pentagon

net for network administrative sites, which are networks running other networks; for example, local Internet gateway servers often are found in this domain

org for organizational sites, such as public and non-profit businesses and groups

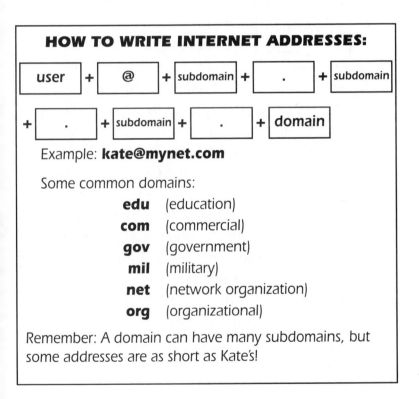

HOW TO WRITE INTERNET ADDRESSES:

user + @ + subdomain + . + subdomain
+ . + subdomain + . + **domain**

Example: **kate@mynet.com**

Some common domains:

edu (education)
com (commercial)
gov (government)
mil (military)
net (network organization)
org (organizational)

Remember: A domain can have many subdomains, but some addresses are as short as Kate's!

Sometimes you will see an address that has something like *edu.uk*. The *uk* means that the address is in England, also known as the **United Kingdom**; *au* means Australia; and *fr* means France. If there is no country code, then it usually means that the site is in the United States.

Or sometimes you will see a subdomain that looks like this: ***mach1.mynet.com***. The ***mach1*** means that it is a subdomain, which means it belongs to another computer that is located within the MyNet local network of computers.

edu.fr

edu.uk

edu.au

"I'm ready to cruise now!" Zack exclaims.

CyberSarge is waiting on the screen, but he is standing in the corner. "Let's see how much you've learned. Don't worry kids, I'll be here if you need me."

Today they will use Kate's account to log on to MyNet. Their gateway software—a TCP/IP program supplied by MyNet—is simple. Kate double clicks on the program icon to start it and when the window opens, Kate moves her mouse pointer and clicks on the *Connect* icon.

Since they have already set up their proper telephone numbers and Internet address, Kate and Zack just wait while their modem dials. After a moment they hear the continuous static sound telling them that they have connected. The two modems, theirs and the one at MyNet, figure out how to talk to one another. Then the *Connect* icon changes to a *Disconnect* icon. That means they are online! When they want to leave the Internet, they will click on the *Disconnect* icon.

"What's first?" Zack asks his sister.

"Well, like CyberSarge keeps telling us, the best place to start is at the beginning." Kate gives her brother an excited smile. "Let's check to see if we have any e-mail."

Kate clicks on the *e-mail* icon and as the program starts, their first lesson appears on the screen:

File   Edit   View

E-MAIL

Almost all of the e-mail programs do the same things. The problem is that almost all of them do it slightly differently. We're not going to be able to discuss all the various command sequences—or instructions—of every e-mail program. Instead we will look at the basic functions most e-mail programs have in common.

These basic functions are:

1. **READING THE E-MAIL THAT IS SENT TO YOU**

2. **SAVING YOUR E-MAIL TO A FILE ON YOUR COMPUTER** so that you can read it later

3. **PRINTING OUT YOUR E-MAIL** so you can give a hard copy to someone

4. **REPLYING TO YOUR E-MAIL LETTERS**

5. **WRITING BRAND-NEW E-MAIL LETTERS** to send

6. **ATTACHING FILES, PICTURES, OR OTHER OBJECTS TO THE E-MAIL LETTERS** you are sending

7. **SENDING YOUR COMPLETED E-MAIL MESSAGES** on the Internet

8. **KEEPING AN INTERNET ADDRESS BOOK** to make it easier to send e-mail messages to people you write to a lot

That's really all any e-mail program does and all it really needs to do. Some programs make it easier to accomplish these things

than others do. Some have built-in spell checkers, while others don't. Some, like the commercial version of Eudora™, allow you setup **filters** so mail from a particular mailing list or an Internet key pal will automatically be routed into a special mailbox. For example, you could instruct your e-mail program to send every letter from Julie to a special mailbox that you've named **Julie**. Or you could send all letters that have the phrase, kid news, in them to a **kid news** mailbox.

Before you can read or send e-mail, you need to set up your e-mail program so that it can talk to your Internet gateway provider. A program such as Netcom's Netcruiser™ or PSI's Pipeline™ does this automatically when you log on to their service for the first time, so you don't have to do anything.

If you're using another e-mail program, such as Eudora™, then you'll have to do the setup yourself. Eudora™, which is what we're using for this example, needs a few basic pieces of information.

The first step is to click on the **Configuration** menu item. This is what Eudora™ calls it. Some programs may call this **Setup** or **Preferences**.

Now you'll be asked to enter the four basic pieces of information:

1. YOUR POP (OR MAIL) ACCOUNT NAME. This is the Internet address where you get your mail delivered. For Kate this is **_kate@mynet.com_**

2. YOUR REAL NAME. Some Internet addresses can be confusing, such as: **_U913@anynet.com_**. Even with Kate's address, we don't know which Kate it is. There are thousands of Kates on the Internet. Putting in your real name will tell the people receiving your e-mail exactly who you are. (We suggest using the initial of your last name

instead of your entire last name, or your first and
middle names with the initial of your last name.)

3. **YOUR SMTP (OR MAIL SERVER)**. This is essentially
your local Internet postmaster's address. This is usually
something like: ***smtp@mynet.com***. When you sign up
with a service provider they will give you this data.

4. **YOUR RETURN ADDRESS**. This will usually be the
same as your POP address.

Almost every e-mail reader will need this same
information. If you don't know the answers to one of the
questions, a quick call to your service provider should get
you the answer. You should also keep your list with the
information about your Internet gateway server close to
your computer so that you can refer to it whenever the
need arises. [See Chapter 9: Recording Your Internet
Gateway Information, starting on page 161, to find the
logs we provide for just this purpose.]

HARD COPY

This refers to printing out a
paper copy of a computer
document on a printer.

FILTERS

Filters are used by software
programs to send information
to a particular place so you
don't have to do it by hand. It's
just like how a coin sorter
works: You feed any coin into
the opening and the machine
directs the nickels to one slot,
dimes to another, pennies to
another, and so on.

POP

POP stands for Post Office
Protocol. POP is a system that
allows Internet mail servers to
act just like a real post office.
POPs look at the mail that
arrives and route it toward its
final destination.

SMTP

SMTP stands for Simple Mail
Transfer Protocol. SMTP is the
language that Internet mail
servers (or postmasters) use to
talk to one another and to
exchange e-mail letters.

Now that you're set up, you need to send a test message to see if everything is working. The easiest way is to send a note to yourself.

> **To: kate@mynet.com**
> **From: kate@mynet.com**
> **Subject: Test**
> **This message is a test.**
> **>>Kate**

OK. Now that you've written it, let's send it.

Because the Internet is so large, your local mail server or postmaster program only has direct connections with a few other computers on the Net. When e-mail arrives at one of those directly connected computers, the postmaster there checks to see if the person you sent the mail to is at that site. If so, the mail is delivered. Otherwise it is routed on to the other sites that **that** computer is directly connected to; it keeps going from computer to computer until it finds the right one. If you look at the top section of the e-mail you receive (the header), you'll see the routing it took to get your e-mail delivered. At first glance this looks like gibberish, but if you look closer you'll see the computers that your e-mail letter went through to get to you.

In the case of our test letter, since it doesn't have to travel anywhere, it will be delivered instantly.

So click on the file menu item that lets you receive mail. Some programs, like Eudora™, allow you to download your mail and read it later. Others require that you read while you're online. Remember that reading your mail and replying to it offline when you're not hooked up to your Internet gateway, can save you a lot of online time. Since you're often paying for the time that you actually are online, being able to read your e-mail offline can save you money.

So now you've put the mail in a temporary mailbox. After you read it, you usually have a few choices:

1. **KEEP THE LETTER ON YOUR COMPUTER**. Usually you'll do this by storing it in a **Saved Mail** area. Many e-mail programs allow you to set up several "mailboxes" where you store your e-mail letters.

2. **REPLY TO THE LETTER**. You can either do this immediately by clicking on the **Reply** item on the menu, or wait until later when you have more time, write it offline, and then log back on to the Internet to send it.

3. **TRASH THE LETTER**. Just like what you do with your paper mail at home—unless, of course, it's recyclable— you can take e-mail letters you're done with, crumple them up, and toss them in a trash can—only this is an electronic can. Some e-mail programs let you retrieve messages from the trash, at least temporarily. It's like throwing something in the waste basket and then getting it out before it gets dumped into the outside trash can and carried away by the garbage collectors. Usually when you log off, the trash can is cleaned up and your trash disappears forever, so be careful not to throw away something that you may want to look at later!

4. **PRINT THE LETTER**. You can select the **Print** item on the menu to print out a hard copy of the e-mail message on your printer.

5. **SAVE THE LETTER**. You can also save it to a file and open it later in your word processor. Almost every e-mail program will have these two options.

6. **SET UP AN ADDRESS BOOK**. Finally, most e-mail programs will allow you to set up an address book in

which you can enter the Internet addresses of the people you write to most often. It's much simpler to select an address from a list than to type it in each and every time. This is because each time you type something in you might misspell the address and the mail will never be delivered. Most of the time, the mail server will return the e-mail letter to you as undeliverable—just like the real post office—but sometimes it will just vanish into cyberspace.

"There's one other thing that e-mail lets you do," CyberSarge says. "E-mail lets you subscribe to mailing lists."

"I've heard about mailing lists," says Zack, nodding. "But I don't totally understand them."

"Mailing lists operate in two ways. The first way is through newsgroup newsletters," replies CyberSarge. "It's like subscribing to a magazine. Once you subscribe to a magazine, it pops up in your Internet mailbox once a day, or once a month—depending upon how often it gets published. You usually do not participate in writing or putting together the information that it provides."

"I know what the second way is," Kate pipes in. "It's when a group of people who are interested in the same subject start a newsgroup discussion group."

"Right. And to join these discussion groups you need to be added to a mailing list as you would with any other newsgroup. All the messages go into a listserver and then get sent to everyone on the mailing list."

"What's a listserver?" asks Zack.

"That's an important question, and it's also our next lesson!" exclaims CyberSarge. The screen begins to scroll:

File	Edit	View

LISTSERVER MAILING LISTS

What is a Listserver mailing list? Quite simply, it is a list of people who share a similar interest and want to receive and/or exchange messages in newsgroups, discussion groups, and bulletin boards. Listserver mailing lists are maintained by an automated postmaster, or Listserv program.

Anyone can subscribe to a list by sending a **Subscribe** command to the **Listserv** address. Any e-mail letter sent to the list's address is copied and mass-mailed to the e-mail mailbox of every person who subscribed to the list.

When using Listservers you have to remember there are two different addresses.

1. The **list address** is the address you send something to if you want it to be sent to everyone else who has subscribed to the list. This address would look like: ***baseball@mynet.com*** if the subject was baseball.

2. The **Listserv** address is the address you send all of your commands to and would look like: ***listserv@mynet.com.***

The most common commands you might send to a Listserv address include:

A. **Subscribe** to subscribe to the mailing list. This would look like: ***subscribe listname <your User name>***

B. **Unsubscribe** to unsubscribe to a mailing list you have previously subscribed to. This looks like: ***unsubscribe listname***

C. **Get to** a file from the mailing list. This would look like: ***get filename filetype***

D.Index will get you a list of the files that are available on the mailing list: ***index listname***

Always remember to:

1. **SEND YOUR LETTERS TO THE LIST ADDRESS.** This is like a post office sorting machine that distributes mail to everyone on the mailing list. Don't send commands here.

2. **SEND YOUR COMMANDS TO THE LISTSERV ADDRESS**. This is like a postmaster who sends you the document you asked for. Don't send letters here.

"But how do we find what mailing lists are on the Internet?" asks Kate.

"That's not always so easy," replies CyberSarge. "There are so many of them. One of the best sources is to subscribe to a newsgroup that talks about mailing lists. Usually they will have an FAQ file you can download to your computer."

"What's an FAQ?" Zack asks CyberSarge.

"FAQ's are usually contained in Usenet newsgroups. And that's part of your next lesson," CyberSarge smiles.

File	Edit	View

USENET NEWSGROUPS AND NEWSREADERS

E-mail is usually "one-to-one," which means you're sending a personal note to a friend on the Internet. Usenet newsgroups are "one-to-many," which means you're posting a message for a lot of people to read.

Usenet newsgroups are international meeting places where people gather to meet their friends, discuss the day's events, keep up with computer trends, or just write about whatever is on their minds.

Taking part in a Usenet discussion can be an exciting experience. Nobody knows what you look or sound like, how old you are, or what your background is. You're judged only on what you have to say, not how you look or how you dress.

The basic building block of Usenet is the newsgroup, which is a collection of messages with a related theme. Currently, there are more than 10,000 of these newsgroups, in several different languages, which talk about everything from art to zoology, from science fiction to knitting.

The main areas of Usenet newsgroups include:

bionet	Research biology
bit.listserv	Conferences originating as Bitnet mailing lists
biz	Business
comp	Computers and related subjects
misc	Discussions that don't fit anywhere else
sci	Science subjects
news	News about Usenet itself
rec	Hobbies, games, and recreation
sci	Science other than research biology

CYBERSARGE SAYS:

Keep track of your time online. You'll have a lot more fun if you know your limits ahead of time—and stick to them! It's very easy to become addicted to online chats and sending messages, and before you know it, your phone bill has skyrocketed. The last thing you want to do is become grounded by your parents because of an enormous phone bill at the end of the month.

FAQ

FAQs are Frequently Asked Questions. They're the best place to start when you're curious about a subject. These files usually end with **.faq**.

soc	Social and cultural issues
talk	Talking about politics and/or other topics, often controversial
alt	Alternative look at subjects
clari	Commercial wire-service stories
k12	Educational subjects for students and teachers

In addition, many servers carry additional newsgroups for their particular city, state, or region. For example, the **_pnw.general_** newsgroup is a discussion group where people who live in the Pacific Northwest can find news and information related to that part of the country. Within the Pacific Northwest, Seattle, Portland, and Vancouver have their own city newsgroups. In fact, most of the major cities in the United States have at least one newsgroup.

With all these newsgroups, you're bound to find something that is interesting to you. For a list of USENET NEWSGROUPS FOR KIDS, turn to page 142.

Some newsgroups also contain pictures that you can download. The pictures sometimes appear as binary messages so that they can be sent reliably through computer systems. To turn the pictures into binary messages, they have to be **UUencoded**. When you download the messages, you then have to **UUdecode** from binary files **back** into regular files so that you can actually see the pictures.

Think of this process as if you were a detective sending secret messages. You would encode—put a message into a code—when you put it online; that way, no one but your secret agent friend could understand it. When your secret agent friend downloads the file, he or she would then decode it—take the message out of code and turn it into a readable form.

BINARY

This is a number system that uses only a 1 or 0. It is the system used by computers to transfer files.

PUBLIC DOMAIN

Public domain means that no one owns something, such as some software programs available on the Net. When something is public domain, it is free to anyone who wants to get and use it.

To send a binary file, the sender will UUencode the file and post it on a newsgroup. To receive the file, you download the UUencoded version to your PC or Macintosh™ and **UUdecode** it. Most picture files are not "secret" as in our explanation above, and there are many public domain UUencoders and decoders available on the Internet.

Now that you've decided you want to subscribe to a newsgroup through your service provider, here are the steps, given to you by your provider, that you need to take.

SUBSCRIBING TO A NEWSGROUP

First you need to get a list of the available newsgroups. Not all servers carry all Usenet newsgroups, but most will carry the basic newsgroups.

Then, to read the newsgroups, you need a newsreader software program. There are several different newsreaders available, and it is likely that one was either included in the software package you purchased or provided to you by your local server.

Though they will vary in some ways, every newsreader program will have five basic functions:

1. GET AND UPDATE A LIST OF YOUR AVAILABLE NEWSGROUPS. The first time you select this option on your newsreader program it's probably going to take a while. Downloading a list of up to 10,000 items can be slow. But you should only have to do it once. From then on you can refresh (update) the list by asking for only the new groups that have been added since the last time you checked. (Remember to note the date you downloaded the list the first time so that you can refer back to that date when you want to refresh your list.)

NEWSREADER SOFTWARE PROGRAM

This is a special software program that allows your computer to read the news available in newsgroups. The newsreader software programs usually come with your Internet service package.

CYBERSARGE SAYS:

Remember that the Internet is like being in a public mall. When you're online, show respect for others who are surfing the Net. Don't pollute cyberspace with graffiti or childish behavior.

PASTE

This means clipping sections from one file and putting them into another.

2. **SUBSCRIBE AND UNSUBSCRIBE TO NEWSGROUPS.** You can either scroll through the downloaded list of available newsgroups and tag those you want to read, or—and this second option is faster if you know the group you want—you can just manually type in the name.

3. **READ THE NEWSGROUPS YOU'VE SUBSCRIBED TO**. Depending on your particular newsreader program, you can do this online by scrolling through the list of headers and then clicking on selected ones to read them, or marking the headers offline and then going back online and downloading only those articles you've selected.

4. **REPLY TO AN ARTICLE OR POST A NEW ONE.** This is like using a mailing list. You're sending a message to a group of people who read this newsgroup. It's also like posting a note on your school bulletin board.

5. **SAVE SELECTED ARTICLES TO A FILE.** When you find something you want to keep (like an FAQ—Frequently Asked Question—article on a subject that interests you), then you can save it onto your hard disk as a file. Later you can use your newsreader or a word processing program to read it again, or to print out a copy on your printer.

Some newsreaders will also allow you to read only certain threads that you have chosen, such as a series of articles on a particular subject.

"Are there any rules for posting articles to a newsgroup?" asks Kate.

"Only the Seven Simple Rules," replies CyberSarge, smiling, "and all of these involve common sense and common courtesy."

File   Edit   View

SEVEN SIMPLE RULES FOR NEWSGROUP POSTING

1. POST IT IN THE RIGHT PLACE. Don't post your thoughts on dog training to the Chinese cooking group.

2. DON'T SPAM. We've decided that SPAM stands for **Sending Particularly Annoying Messages**! Spamming is sending an article of yours **everywhere** on the Internet. Instead of sending an article to specific groups that might be interested in it, you send it to anyone and everyone. This is not a nice practice. And some services will penalize you or even take you off their service for doing this. Don't clutter up the Internet with junk mail.

3. KEEP YOUR HEADER SIMPLE AND DIRECT. Don't try to be too cute, just say what your article is about in as few words as possible. You want the people who are interested in what you're talking about to notice, understand, and read your article.

4. SAY WHAT YOU HAVE TO SAY AND THEN STOP. You are busy, and so is everyone else on the Internet. No one has the time to read dozens of pages. Make sure you say what you want to say clearly and in the shortest way possible. Then stop!

5. REFERENCE YOUR MESSAGE TO AN EXISTING THREAD. To do this include a sentence or two from a previous article so the other readers will know what you're talking about. On the other hand, you don't want to paste everything that was previously said on the subject. Referencing is done so that the people coming online in the middle of the discussion will know what you are talking about.

6. **TRY NOT TO SHOUT.** TYPING EVERYTHING IN CAPITAL LETTERS IS CONSIDERED SHOUTING. Don't do it. Use capitals only when you want to emphasize a point. If you type everything in capitals, otherwise known as **caps**, no one will want to read what you have to say.

7. **TREAT PEOPLE JUST LIKE YOU WANT TO BE TREATED.** There will be arguments, and you'll disagree with someone's point of view. You'll even get mad. But once you've posted an angry article, you can't unpost it. Your words will be there for everyone to read—and they'll probably be there for a lot longer than you'd like. Count to ten before making an angry reply. Then think of a way to make a constructive, useful comment instead.

"OK," Kate says. "We can send e-mail and read articles. What if I just want to talk to someone—like I do on the phone—without having to send a letter, even an electronic one. Can I do that?"

"Well," replies CyberSarge. "UNIX™ systems have something called *talk* that is used to let different people chat with one another when they both log on. The Internet takes that one step further. Two or more people can get together on an IRC."

File	Edit	View

INTERNET RELAY CHAT

Internet Relay Chat—or just plain IRC—is a fairly new part of the Internet. IRCs allow you to **chat** in real time with people all over the world, just like you would having a telephone conversation—only this is online.

When using an IRC, remember what time it is in the parts of the world where you're calling. It may be 3:00 in the afternoon where you are, but it could be midnight in your friend's city. Schedule a reasonable time for both of you when setting up an IRC chat.

IRCs became really popular during the Persian Gulf War. People used IRCs to catch up on news updates from around the world that came across the wire. News updates were broadcast on a single channel and people would gather on that channel to read the news reports.

People like IRCs because they let you chat worldwide from any site that is connected to the Internet. Any computer user can connect to an IRC server and communicate with anybody anywhere in the world—right now. It's like having a telephone conference call with people in Russia, Mexico, and Australia—all at the same time!

One of the main attractions of IRC is that you can create and control your own channels. You can have private online chats with a group of friends, like getting together at someone's house—only this house is on the Internet in cyberspace and your guests may be from all over the world!

If you aren't using one of the Internet programs that supports IRC, you can get both Windows™ and Macintosh™ shareware programs from several FTP sites on the Internet.

REAL TIME

Real time refers to actual time. In terms of the Internet, it means that you can get an instant response to whatever you do. Think of how you speak on the phone versus how you send a paper letter through snail mail; when you're on the phone you get instant responses from the person on the other end—in real time—to whatever you say. When you send a paper letter through snail mail, you have to wait for it to get picked up by the postal carrier, taken to the post office, and delivered before you can get a response.

SHAREWARE

Shareware is like freeware and it doesn't cost you anything to get and try it out—but if you like it and want to use it, then the author of the program asks for a small fee.

TROJANS

Like the Trojan Horse in Greek mythology, trojan programs are tiny little programs hidden inside larger regular programs. And like the Trojan warriors, they are often hidden there to do nasty things to your computer, such as erasing files on your computer.

After you install an IRC program and configure it—following the instructions that come with the program—you must now choose your **nickname**. This is the name (**not** your full, real name) by which you'll be known on the chat channels.

Then you call up your Internet provider as you normally do and log on to an IRC Server. [There is a list of IRC servers included in Chapter 7: Guide to the Galaxy, starting on page 124.]

Once you have logged on, your Server may give you some rules or warnings, such as "Flaming will NOT be tolerated" or "Watch out for Trojans." Trojans are tiny programs that can hide in other programs and do damage to computers that access them.

Before you know it, you'll be online and chatting with a group of Internauts from all over the world.

Much of what you see may look like gibberish, and a lot of things will be hard to understand. Don't worry about it. Like much of the Internet, the gibberish parts don't matter, and the stuff you really need to understand will become more clear the more time you spend online.

Here is a sample conversation from one of the IRCs. As you will see, it all happens very fast. Different people are logged on all at the same time, different conversations take place at once, people talk to each other people and comment on other people's conversations. It's fast and thrilling to participate in a chat because you never know who's going to say what next! In the following example, we changed the names to protect the innocent. (But we didn't correct any of the spelling errors!)

[SERVER]	**Deon@aol.com** has joined this channel
[Deon]	hi, I'm me
[marie]	bn: hello! deon:hello!
[tranh]	hi deon

[SERVER]	stan!stan@indyunix.iupui.edu has joined this channel
[marie]	Margie: O wow!
[bn]	marie: are you going to cg tonite `-)
[deon]	what's cg?
[bn]	it's a secret
[marie]	tell him
[deon]	tell me
[bn]	can't, it's a secret
[deon]	later to all of you
[M&M]	Deon: Did you have karma or rua dweeb?
[tranh]	ptr, :)))
[SERVER]	Deon has quit IRC have fun don't fight
[bn]	who's going to cg tonite?
[ptr]	tranh: I see.....
[marie]	Margie: what do you think?
[bn]	marie: good!!! it's a date then!
[Marie]	not. LJBF
[grrl]	Hello everybody
[bn]	hi grrl
[Margie]	marie: do u think he's realyl really mad?
[SERVER]	PeJay@cybot.westwords.calstate.edu has joined this channel
[PeJay]	hello out there
[phyl]	stan: LTNS!
[stan]	phyl: i don't irc lately
[Margie]	marie: shocked :-o
[bn]	stan's a shybernaut
[stan]	LOL
[Aron]	_Margie_ Have you found any new commands?
[Margie]	yup :-)
[grrl]	hello from Israel!!!!!!
[stan]	phyl what you been up to???
[phyl]	oops, gotta go! e-mail me stan!
[SERVER]	phyl has left this channel

CYBERSARGE SAYS:

When you see an address that takes up more than one line in this book, such as:

http://www.state.com/city/street.html

it should be typed out on one line with no spaces where the line breaks. Remember there are never any spaces in Internet addresses.

> [MAXX]   hello grrl, Canada here
> [bn]   marie...u still there?

As you can read, it looks like **they** know what they're talking about. But it's hard for anybody else to figure out!

In a way, logging on to a channel on the IRC is like going to a party where you don't know anybody. Groups of people stand around talking, but you feel awkward. The secret is to listen in for a while. Maybe the people are talking about something you're interested in. Then just introduce yourself, using your nickname as we talked about earlier, such as "Hi, I'm Hoagie"—or Juicy or MC Cyber or Dweeboid—whatever name you've chosen.

Maybe someone will say hello. Or maybe not. See what happens.

Another thing you can do is to talk with people you **do** know. With IRC you can set up your own channel, and arrange—by e-mail, snail mail, or telephone—with other members of your family in other states or across the world, with a friend, or with a bunch of friends to join you online at a certain specific time.

The first person to join a channel becomes that channel's operator and waits for others to join the channel. The channel operator can set the channel mode to private and allow users to join only by invitation. You and your friends or family can have a private meeting or chat in that channel without intrusion from other users. One benefit of this is obvious: no long-distance toll calls! Another is that you won't get strange interruptions from people you don't know, don't particularly care to know, or even would like to avoid!

"Wow!" Zack looks at Kate. "We gotta try this IRC thing. It sounds great! It's cool to chat with lots of different people at the same time. And it looks like you have to respond pretty quickly!"

"Yes, chats develop at a pretty rapid pace, but you can just lurk if you want to before joining in," says CyberSarge.

"I like the idea of lurking," says Kate. "That way I can see if the conversation is one I want to join or if I just want to hang out and watch."

"Yes, chats are fun!" agrees CyberSarge. "So far you've logged on to your server, read your e-mail, and subscribed to newsgroups. Let's assume you've even had an IRC session. What I'd like to do next is talk about Telnet. It's another great resource on the Internet."

File	Edit	View

TELNET

Telnet is an Internet program that lets you log on to another computer and use it as if it were your own computer. You can also do this with just a modem and an old fashioned communications program.

The difference with Telnet on the Internet is that you can log on to a computer in Spain for the price of a local phone call!

Using Telnet, you type commands onto your keyboard that are then sent from your computer to the local Internet service provider. Then the commands are sent from your provider to the remote computer that you want to access. It's as though you had a giant mainframe sitting on your desk and are running it from your keyboard. Cool, huh?

With Telnet you can browse through directories, connect into huge databases to do research, or even log

CYBERSARGE SAYS:

There are two forms of mailing lists on the Internet.

The first is newsletter newsgroups. Joining these is like subscribing to a magazine: You get updates automatically and usually do not participate in writing the information you get.

The second are newsgroup discussion groups, where you can post messages and respond to other messages with people who are interested in the same subject that you are interested in. [Refer to graph on page 86.]

LURKING

Lurking is hanging around in the background and watching online discussions without getting involved. Most of us are lurkers when we first enter a new site on the Internet.

on to libraries around the world to check if they have a certain book that you are looking for.

One downside to all this is that when you Telnet to another computer, you have to use the menus that are set up on that system. They can be a bit strange and unfamiliar, so you're often learning by trial and error.

Most Telnet computers will require you to have an account. But they may also let you log on as **guest** or **newuser**.

Once you're accepted into their system, follow the menus to look around—and ask for help when you need it. You will not be able to access all the information on these computers because they only make part of their information available to Internet users. This is because these computers are part of a larger organization, such as a university. And university networks only let teachers and students who have an account at that university log on to most of the databases. But they do make available their libraries and other services to Internet users who log on as guests.

Computers accessible by Telnet are plugged into the Internet to make certain services available to anyone. Their addresses look a lot like regular Internet addresses, but they have more numbers in them. For example, this is what a Telnet address looks like:

computer.myschool.edu199.18.22.8

Here are the six basic steps to having a successful Telnet session:

1. **START UP YOUR TELNET PROGRAM.**

2. **GIVE THE PROGRAM THE ADDRESS** where you want to connect.

3. **LOG ON TO THE REMOTE COMPUTER.**

4. **SET UP THE TERMINAL EMULATION—** you'll find this in the online Telnet set up

directions—so you can see what the remote computer is saying on your computer screen. Otherwise you may only see a lot of strange characters as if you're reading a foreign language. The most common terminal emulation setting is called **VT100**, which is the standard for terminal-based communications.

5. NOW THAT YOU'RE LOGGED ON to the system, you can look and play around on the remote computer. Unless you have a special password, the public password will only let you get into those areas that are public, so you can't do any real harm if you make a mistake.

6. WHEN YOU'RE ALL DONE—QUIT.

When you first log on through Telnet, go to the **Help** menu and find the "escape" character. Make a note of this character so you can get out of the remote computer if you get stuck in a loop. Remember that this system may not use the same keyboard shortcuts that are on your own computer. And while you are logged on to a remote computer, you're playing by that system's rules.

"Telnet is really that simple—and can be that confusing," says CyberSarge. "Often being on Telnet is like being a stranger in a strange place."

"But once you get the hang of it, you can access a lot of great research information from remote computers, such as a university's library, right?" asks Kate.

"You got it!" CyberSarge exclaims.

"So I can use Telnet to log on to another computer and download software?" asks Zack. "My friend Peter told me about this totally hot game on a computer in a university in Michigan."

"Yes," CyberSarge responds. "That's one thing you

TERMINAL EMULATION

This is a setting on Telnet computers that allows your computer to translate what the remote Telnet computer is saying. You choose the terminal emulation setting from the menu provided from the Telnet site you are logged on to.

ESCAPE CHARACTER

An escape character is a keyboard command that allows you to exit a computer system in case that system crashes or gets into a loop.

LOOP

A computer loop is what happens when you get into a series of repeating commands, so you end up running around in endless circles. This usually causes your computer to crash or freeze, meaning that you have to restart your computer to get it running again.

can do with Telnet. But a better way to transfer files
or download is through FTP."

File	Edit	View

FTP

FTP stands for **F**ile **T**ransfer **P**rotocol. FTP allows you to
access remote computers and retrieve files from these
computers. You can find FTP in the menu of your Internet
access software program.

What sort of files are available through FTP?
Well, there are hundreds of systems connected
to the Internet that have file libraries, or
archives, accessible to the public. Much of
the material in these file libraries consists
of free or low-cost programs for almost
every kind of computer. If you want a
different communications program for your
IBM™ or Macintosh™, or if you feel like playing a
new game, you'll probably be able to get it using FTP.

There are also huge libraries of online documents as
well. Copies of historical documents, from the Magna
Carta to the Declaration of Independence, are also yours
for the downloading. You can also find song lyrics,
poems, even summaries of every episode ever made of
your favorite animated TV series. You can also find
extensive files detailing everything you could possibly
want to know about the Internet itself.

The basic steps in any FTP session are:

1. START UP YOUR FTP PROGRAM.

2. GIVE YOUR FTP PROGRAM THE ADDRESS you
want to connect to.

3. When you connect to the remote computer,
IDENTIFY YOURSELF with your user name. If you
don't have an account, try to log on as ***guest***.

4. TELL THE REMOTE SITE YOUR PASSWORD if you have an account there, or try **guest** again.

5. USE THE REMOTE COMPUTER'S HELP MENUS for instructions on how to move around through the directories.

6. CHANGE DIRECTORIES AND LOOK AROUND FOR FILES you might want to download.

7. SET THE TRANSFER MODE WHEN YOU FIND A FILE you do want to download. This is usually ASCII for plain text files, or binary for other types of files, like programs and pictures.

8. DOWNLOAD THE FILE you want, then continue to search for and download other files.

9. FINALLY, QUIT WHEN YOU'RE ALL DONE.

Chances are you won't have an account with the remote computer site. So how do you log on as guest or visitor? Almost all remote computer sites that allow outside access use the user identification **anonymous**.

By using the name **anonymous**, you are telling that FTP site that you aren't a regular user of that site, but you would still like to access that FTP site, look around, and retrieve files.

So, when your FTP program asks for **User**, you will type in the word: **anonymous**.

Now you need to enter your password. If you log on as **anonymous**, you need to use your full Internet address for your password. Kate would type in: **kate@mynet.com**.

Many FTP programs will allow you to set up using **anonymous** and your password together, so you only have to do it once. If your FTP program doesn't allow this, you will have to enter both each time once you've made contact with the remote computer.

CYBERSARGE SAYS:

If you try to go into a directory where you aren't supposed to be, you'll either be asked for a password or not allowed into that directory. FTP sites are like hotels; everyone can use the public areas such as the lobby, restaurant, and shops, but you have to have a key to get into one of the rooms.

DIRECTORIES

The hard disk on your computer is divided into directories. Each directory can contain many different files. If you think of your computer's hard disk like a file cabinet, then directories are drawers in that cabinet.

ASCII

ASCII is a nickname for **A**merican **S**tandard **C**ode for **I**nformation **I**nterchange, and was created so that there would be a standard language to transfer files between different types of programs and computers. That standard language consists of plain text only. You pronounce it "ask-key."

BIT

Computers store all information in a binary system that consists of bits. A bit is the smallest unit of information in a computer, and is either a 1 or a 0.

BYTE

A byte is a group of eight bits.

README FILES

Readme files are text files, often found on FTP sites, that explain what is in an FTP directory or that provide other useful information. You also get readme files with computer software, often explaining things you need to know that are not in the printed instruction manual.

Once you're logged on to the FTP computer, you will normally find yourself in the main directory. If there is a readme file, you can download it into your computer as an ASCII, or plain text, file and read it on your computer screen without exiting. This file will usually tell you something about the files available at this site.

Most public files are located in a directory named PUB. To get there you will enter: ***cd/pub***.

You can use the **cd** command, which stands for **change directory**, to travel up and down through the remote computer site's directories until you get to where you want to be. It's kind of like riding in an elevator. You can also double-click your mouse pointer on the **parent** directory to move up, or on, one item in the lists of subdirectories to move down.

When you've decided to get a file—in other words to download it to your computer—you should usually use the binary option. If you download a program file in ASCII format, you won't be able to use it. A good rule is to always use the binary option, unless you're just going to look at a readme or index file. Your program will tell you how to choose one or the other.

"Up till now," CyberSarge says as he reappears on the computer screen, "you've been going one-on-one with a remote computer."

"Yeah," agrees Zack. "We can log off from one remote computer and log on to another anywhere in the world. That's great. But it seems kind of slow."

"Is there a better way?" asks Kate.

"I thought you'd never ask," smiles CyberSarge. "One of the best ways to search for information on almost any subject is through Gopherspace."

File	Edit	View

GOPHERSPACE

Gopher™ was developed at the University of Minnesota, which is one of the reasons for its name: The Minnesota football team is named the Gophers.

Gopher™ is a menu-driven program that allows you to hop around the world looking for information through the Internet. Like a real gopher that burrows through the ground seeking out buried treasures, Gopher™ burrows through cyberspace—which, in the case of Gophers, is often called Gopherspace.

Gopher programs are designed to search through Gopher servers around the world for the information you're looking for. You can jump from one Gopher server to another by simply clicking on items on the Gopher™ menu. When you find a document that interests you, you can read it online or save it to your computer to read later.

Gopher servers contain all kinds of interesting and helpful information. For example, some libraries and bookstores maintain Gopher servers with information about the books they carry. Other Gopher servers have been set up to carry documents on a particular subject, like medicine or baseball.

Gopher programs can be used with another program, called Veronica, which allows you to search for Gopher menus anywhere on the Internet based on key words. We'll

CYBERSARGE SAYS:

Don't get too impatient when waiting for something to happen and start pressing the enter key. This is like honking when you're stalled in traffic; it won't get you there any faster.

GOPHER SERVER

A Gopher server is a computer on the Internet that is set up to service the information requests issued by a Gopher program. Gopher programs—also called **search engines**—help you find information you are looking for in cyberspace.

BOOKMARKS

Bookmarks are markers that allow you to mark a Gopher menu or file that you like so you can return to that menu or file whenever you want. All of your bookmarks are kept in a booklist that acts just like your own personal Gopher menu.

discuss Veronica and other search engines in the next chapter.

Gopher is really just an organizing tool, like the table of contents in a book that directs you to the chapter you are most interested in.

When you start up the Gopher program on your computer, it will display a list—often called a Gopher menu—of Gopher servers that are available to be searched. You then pick the Gopher server that you want to go to. For example, if you go to the University of Washington's Gopher server you would see a list of the documents available to you on the University's Gopher server.

Gophers are very popular because they are very easy to use.

But because they are so popular, using a Gopher can often be slow because so many people are trying to use the same Gopher server at the same time. One trick to remember is that when it's daytime in the United States, it's nighttime in Europe. Pick a Gopher server in England or Italy for your search and it may go much faster. On the Internet, calling overseas is the same as the cost of a local call!

Suppose you find a really neat Gopher menu. Gopherspace—or cyberspace in general—is so huge, you may not remember how to get back there. You can't leave bread crumbs or pebbles to mark the path. But you can leave a **bookmark**.

Each Gopher program has its own particular bookmark commands, but they all work on the same basic principle: You leave a bookmark in the program's booklist. Your booklist acts just like a regular Gopher menu and by clicking on one of the menu items, you instantly jump to that Gopher menu you visited a day—or a month—ago.

"I think I'm going to like gophering!" exclaims Kate, who already has a list of things she wants to look up. "It's a great way to find out information for my homework assignments."

"And they seem really easy to use," adds Zack.

"Gophers really *are* easy to use," CyberSarge assures them. "The people who designed the Gopher™ system knew that the students and teachers who would be searching through Gopherspace were not necessarily going to be computer wizards, so they wanted to make the program simple."

"I just wish there were more pictures in Gopherspace," Zack says wistfully.

"If it's pictures you want, you have to go to the Web," says CyberSarge.

"Yeah, we talked about the Web a little already, didn't we?" asks Kate. [See Chapter 1: Life on the Internet, page 35.]

"Yes we did. Good memory!" replies CyberSarge. "The Web, as you already know, is what most people call the World Wide Web. That's our next destination."

File   Edit   View

THE WORLD WIDE WEB

The World Wide Web—also known as **WWW** or **the Web**—is the newest and most significant development on the Internet. It is the fastest growing part of the Internet as well as the most user-friendly. The Web can contain your text, pictures, sound, and even video information where many of the other Internet services are limited to text only. You can think of the Web as a place where anyone can publish electronic magazine pages. Then any computer on the Internet equipped with a Web browser software program can view these pages. Think of the Web as the pages in a magazine, which have pictures and text just like in a regular magazine. It's the newest form of electronic publishing on the Internet today!

In Gopherspace, Gopher menus are linked together and a whole world of information can be explored through just a few keystrokes. It's like reading one magazine in the library, finding an article that interests you, returning that magazine, and then checking out another one to read. Amazingly, the World Wide Web is even faster once you figure out how to get around.

Now imagine that instead of going from one menu, or magazine, to another, you can go from one article in a geography magazine to another in a magazine about history—instantly.

For example, you could be reading about American Presidents in one document when you see the name of Thomas Jefferson appear as a key word. Rather than going to another menu through Gopherspace, you could simply click on that key word with your mouse, and you

HIGHLIGHTED

Highlighted means that a word or phrase is marked so that it stands out. The word might be in *italics* or **bolded**. On the Web highlighted words and phrases are hyperlinks that can take you to other locations.

would be automatically taken to a new document that talks about the life of Jefferson. And this new document would have key words that could take you to still more documents, which might be located anywhere in the world. For instance, you might learn that Jefferson spent time in France. If you find that interesting, **France** would become a key word for you. **France** might be highlighted and you could click on it, and jump to a document about **France**. And all this with just a touch of your keyboard or the click of your mouse!

Is this magic? No. It's all based on hypertext. Using hypertext you select a highlighted word—usually by clicking on it with a mouse—and you are taken into an entirely new document.

The World Wide Web is based on hypertext. It is possible for you to go roaming around the Web, bouncing from document to document, using nothing but the key word links in those documents.

Just as you access Gopherspace through a Gopher server, you access the Web through something called a **Web browser**. [For information on Web browsers, see Chapter 1: Life on the Internet, page 36.]

Most Web browsers can read documents **and** can also download them to your computer's hard disk. Web browsers can access files by FTP, they can read Usenet newsgroups, and they can Telnet into remote computer sites. In short, Web browsers let you travel through cyberspace and do almost everything you want.

What is really so special about the Web is that the Web does all of this without you having to know the exact address of where you are, or even how you got there!

The Web is able to accomplish all of this by using something called URLs—**U**niversal **R**esource **L**ocators. URLs are addresses for the location of any Internet resource.

URL

URLs—or **U**niversal **R**esource **L**ocators—are addresses for the location of any type of Internet resource, whether it is a single file on an FTP site, an entire Gopher server, or an image on the Web. URLs do all of this without you having to know the exact address of where you are, or even how you got there! Note that URLs are case sensitive, which means that uppercase letters are considered different from lowercase letters; Library, with a capital "L," is not the same as library with a small "l." So be careful when typing in URL addresses.

CYBERSARGE SAYS AGAIN:

When you see an address that takes up more than one line in this book, such as:

http://www.state.com/city/ street.html

it should be typed out on one line with no spaces where the line breaks. Remember there are never any spaces in Internet addresses.

HYPERTEXT MARKUP LANGUAGE

HyperText Markup Language is the programming language used to create hyperlinks on the Web.

The idea behind URLs was to create a universal system for accessing information on the Internet, no matter if it's a single file on an FTP site, an entire Gopher server, or an image on the Web. That means that when browsing the Web, you're going to have to get used to seeing and typing in things such as:

http://www.library.edu/books/pages.html

The **http** means you're dealing with a Web resource. It stands for **H**yper**T**ext **T**ransport **P**rotocol. HTTP is just a coding system for marking up documents with little markers that change the way the information is seen on the screen.

For instance, if you write a document and place it in a file, then send it to a site on the Web, you need to format the document with the proper HTTP markers so that anyone else on the Web can read it no matter what kind of computer or program they are using. You don't need to learn HTTP markers unless you decide to write your own home page.

Next comes the name of the site on which the resource is located; here that is *www.library* indicating World Wide Web library.

Then you find directories and subdirectories listed in the address. In this address, that is: *edu/books/pages.* For instance, *pages* is a subdirectory of *books* which is a subdirectory of *edu*. *edu* is the overall education directory at the WWW library.

By the way, URL addresses are case sensitive, so be careful when typing them. *Library*, with a capital "L," is **not** the same as *library* with a small "l."

In the above address, notice how the last item ends in *.html*. That stands for **H**yper**T**ext **M**arkup **L**anguage.

You'll find a lot of Web addresses ending in *.html*. Sometimes if you are trying to reach a service without a main HTML page (a gopher server, for example), you may have to end the address with a slash, which looks like this **/** . For instance:

gopher://gopher.mynet.org/

Luckily you will have to type in these long names only once, the first time you go to a new address. Once you add a particular address to your bookmark list, then you can instantly jump to it by just clicking on the name in your list.

"I can't wait to browse the Web," announces Zack as the lesson ends. Kate's broad smile is a clear sign that she's as excited as her little brother.

"OK, Cadets," says CyberSarge. "I think you know enough to try your wings. Now it's time for you two to start navigating the Net and see how much you've learned!"

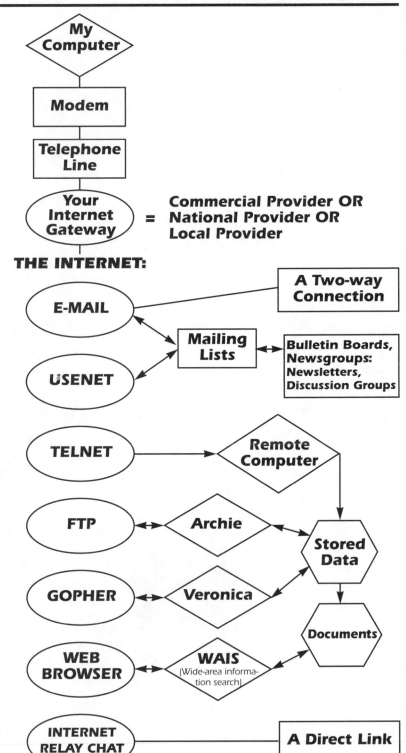

TOOLS

E-MAIL lets you send and receive messages to other computers AND it lets you access Internet magazines and bulletin boards.

USENET accesses newsgroups and discussion groups on almost every subject under the sun.

TELNET allows you to log on to a remote computer.

FTP allows you to transfer files between your computer and a remote computer.

GOPHER lets you search for, read, and copy documents from several computers at once.

WEB BROWSER lets you search for, read, and download documents, photos, sound, and video from all computers that are part of the World Wide Web.

INTERNET RELAY CHATS (IRC) allow you to "chat" in real time with many people all at once via a direct link to computers all over the world.

Chapter 4

Navigating the Internet:

How Do I Get Around in Cyberspace?

Kate and Zack are feeling excited right before their first cruise onto the Net. But Zack is a little worried.

"The Internet is so big," Zack tells his sister. "Even with everything we have learned, how do you find anything out there in cyberspace?"

"Let's ask CyberSarge," replies Kate as she boots up their computer.

When CyberSarge appears on the screen it is clear that he has anticipated their question. "The first time you go onto the Net," he tells them, "it will be an awesome experience. But now you're thinking that cyberspace is a strange space, and you won't really know how to find anything once you get there."

"How did you know?" asks Kate. It seems to her that CyberSarge can practically read their minds! "We're barely logged on to the Internet, and already we feel lost."

"Well, you're not alone," CyberSarge replies comfortingly. "And fortunately there are some tools to help you navigate the Net."

CyberSarge steps aside as the next lesson scrolls across the screen:

File	Edit	View

ARCHIE AND FTP

Using FTP you can download all kinds of documents and software programs from all over the world. The problem is that there are thousands of FTP sites. So how do you find that file on "how to improve your baseball game" that you've heard is out there?

Well, that's where you need the Archie program.

Archie is a computer program that lets you type in search words to search for things. You can use Archie to search through thousands of FTP databases all over the world for the file or files that contain the information you are looking for.

Most FTP directories have a special file that is called an **Index file.** The Index file is a list of what information is contained in each file on that particular computer. Think of an Index file like the index at the back of a book that tells you where in the book to go to find out about a particular subject or to find out the definition of a particular word.

The Archie catalog maintains a list of about 1500 FTP sites where almost 3 million unique files are kept. These files contain over 200 gigabytes of information.

Archie can search this database for file locations when you give it a key word to search for. The Archie program won't actually get the file for you, but it **will** tell you where you can find it. Once you know the file's name and location, you can use your FTP program to get it.

SEARCH WORDS

Documents contain specific words in them that tell you a bit about the subject they are discussing. For example, if you use the search words **baseball**, **pitcher**, and **World Series**, you would find documents that have those words in them. Chances are that a document that has all three of those words would be about World Series baseball pitchers.

ARCHIE

Archie is a computer software program that lets you type in a key word to search for things. You can use Archie to search thousands of FTP databases all over the world for the file or files which contain the information you are looking for.

GIGABYTE

A gigabyte is a billion bytes. A gigabyte looks like 1,000,000,000 bytes.

There are three ways that you can use Archie:

1. **YOU CAN USE AN ARCHIE SERVER THAT IS RUNNING ON YOUR LOCAL INTERNET SERVICE PROVIDER'S SYSTEM.**

2. **YOU CAN USE TELNET TO CONNECT DIRECTLY TO AN ARCHIE SERVER.** Archie servers in the United States include:

> *archie@archie.rutgers.edu*
> *archie@archie.unl.edu*
> *archie@archie.internic.net*
> *archie@archie.ans.net*
> *archie@archie.sura.net*

Let's imagine for this example that you are searching for information about the Apollo 13 space flight mission. When you've logged on, you start your search by typing:

find apollo 13

After Archie has finished its search it will print its results on your screen. The results would not be entire documents, but addresses of where those documents can be found. If Kate wanted to get the Archie server to e-mail these results to her, she would type in: *mail kate@mynet.com*

(You would type in **mail** followed by your own Internet address.)

You can leave your Telnet session by typing **<quit>** or clicking your mouse on the menu item **Quit**.

WILDCARD

Like the joker in a deck of playing cards, a wildcard is used in a computer search. Usually a wildcard is represented by an *. For instance, **go*** means that the search will find every word that starts with go and ends with anything: **go**, such as **going**, **got**, **golf**, etc. As you see from this example you have to be careful using wildcards in searches or you'll end up finding a lot of things you weren't looking for. You usually use a wildcard if you don't have the subject of your search narrowed down yet.

3. YOU CAN USE ARCHIE BY SENDING AN E-MAIL
LETTER DIRECTLY TO AN ARCHIE SERVER. To
conduct an Archie search via e-mail, you should send
an e-mail letter to the Archie server closest to you.
Assuming you were still searching for information
about Apollo 13, in the body of your letter you would
type: *find apollo 13*
> *set mail to kate@mynet.com*
> *quit*

As you might imagine, Archie servers are very busy, so
sending an e-mail request is sometimes faster than trying
to search online.

"OK," says Zack. "I can use Archie to find a file on
an FTP computer site. But how about looking for
something in Gopherspace?"

"Well, then," smiles CyberSarge, "you're going to
need to use Veronica."

| File | Edit | View |

VERONICA IN GOPHERSPACE

Roaming through Gopherspace can be fun. But it can
also be frustrating. You're going to want to find the
document you're looking for without having to jump
around Gopher sites all over the world. Archie can search
FTP sites, so what can we use to search Gopher sites?

The answer is: Veronica.

Veronica is a search tool that you can access through
your Gopher program. Veronica allows you to quickly
scan Gopherspace for particular files and directories.

Veronica asks you to enter a key word. Then it searches
through a database of thousands of Gopher servers for
files and directories whose titles contain your key word.
Finally Veronica puts the results of the search into a

temporary Gopher menu that you can browse through just like a regular Gopher menu.

Veronica lets you choose between two types of searches:

1. **SEARCH GOPHERSPACE BY TITLE WORD(S)** will list every file and directory whose title contains your search words. In this case you can go directly to one of the documents.

2. **FIND ONLY DIRECTORIES BY TITLE WORD(S)** will list only the menus of the Gopher sites that have titles containing your search words. In this case you have to visit each of the Gopher sites to look at the documents.

If you are using a very common word as your search word—such as **Internet**, **kids**, or **history**—you should use the **only directories** type of search. Otherwise you may get back more results than you can handle.

Think through exactly what you want to find and then select search words—also known as **key words**—that will narrow your search as much as possible.

CYBERSARGE SAYS:

While the most simple form of a Veronica search is the use of a single key word, that could get you a menu of over a thousand choices. A better way is to use several key words for your search using the logical operators and, or *and* not. *For example, if you were looking for a listing of this book on Cyberwalk, MCA/Universal's home page, you would type in the key words:* internet children.

"Archie lets us search through the files themselves, but Veronica only lets us search for the titles of documents," says Kate.

"Often just getting the titles is enough," replies CyberSarge, "especially if the people who created the documents gave them a proper title so you'd know what was in the document. But there is a way to search for words or phrases contained *in* the documents. That's called WAIS."

"WAIS?" asks Zack. "What does that stand for?"

"Wide-Area Information Search," replies CyberSarge.

File   Edit   View

WAIS

Wide-Area Information Search is another program for zeroing in on information hidden inside Gopherspace. In a WAIS, the program worries about how to access information located in hundreds of different databases. You give a WAIS a search word and it scans the Net looking for places where your search word is mentioned.

When you start a WAIS, the program will give you a list of which databases you can search. You can select one or more databases for your search.

WAIS will give you a menu of documents, each ranked according to which document best fits your criteria. A "score" of 1,000 is given to the document that contains the most occurrences of your search word. A document with a score of 500 would contain only half as many occurrences.

"What about searching the World Wide Web?" asks Kate.

"There are several sophisticated search engines for the Web," replies CyberSarge. "And new ones are being invented every day. Here are some."

File   Edit   View

FINDING IT ON THE WEB

The Web Crawler is a sophisticated Web search engine that not only returns titles and Web addresses to you when you conduct a search, but also gives you an index of document contents. You can reach Web Crawler at the University of Washington at the following Web address:

http://www/biotech.washington.edu/WebCrawler /Home.html

Lycos is another ambitious Web hunter that resides at Carnegie-Mellon University and can be reached at:

http://lycos.cs.cmu.edu

Lycos has two databases you can search. One contains about 250,000 entries, while the larger database has over 2 million entries.

These are only two of a dozen Web search engines currently available. You can probably reach one or more of these search engines through the default home page in your Web browser program.

CyberSarge says, "Now it's time to really get started. Training is nearing an end, and you guys are ready to blast off into cyberspace!"

"You mean, we're going to actually surf the Net?" Zack is not sure his ears are working correctly.

"Yippee!" Kate yells.

"OK, now let's start from the beginning. You're going to take a short tour of the Net, and I'm going to watch over your shoulder. Keep it really simple this first time," CyberSarge warns. "You're on your own for the first time just to get the feel of it. I'll watch but I'm not going to jump in. So blast off, kids!"

Zack decides to go back to his school's computer lab. They have an Internet connection. Once there he can try out what he's learned. He'll send an e-mail letter to his sister.

Zack turns on the school computer and brings up their Internet program. It's a bit different than the screen on his computer at home, but Cybersarge told him ahead of time not to worry about the little differences. "All the programs do the same things, so you can usually figure them out if you take your time."

Zack sees a mailbox icon and clicks on it. Now a smaller screen opens in the middle of the big screen. At the top is a box that says **TO:** which he knows is where the address goes. He types in:

kate@mynet.com

The box below says **SUBJECT:** Zack types in: *my first e-mail letter*

Now there is a bigger box which is empty. That's where he writes his letter. He types in: *dear kate: this is my first e-mail letter. hope you get it. zack*

All done. He clicks on the little icon that shows a postman delivering mail. This sends the letter out into the Internet, and—he hopes—into Kate's e-mail mailbox.

When Zack comes back home from school he finds Kate busy at the computer. She tells him that she got his letter, and that she has sent him a reply. "But now I'm looking for information on Moby Dick for a book report. I've heard there's a copy of the book on the Internet."

Kate starts her Gopher tour at *gopher.tc.umn.edu* —a Gopher site at the University of Minnesota, which is the home of Gopher. "But it really doesn't matter where you start," she explains to Zack. "As long as you are in Gopherspace, you have access to the same information that everyone else has."

On the screen, the main Gopher menu appears:

- 📁 **Information About Gopher**
- 📁 **Computer Information**
- 📁 **Discussion Groups**
- 📁 **Fun & Games**
- 📁 **Libraries**
- 📁 **News**
- 📁 **Other Gopher and Information Servers**
- 📁 **Phone Books**
- 🔍 **Search Gopher Titles at the University of Minnesota**
- 🔍 **Search lots of places at the University of Minnesota**
- 📁 **University of Minnesota Campus Information**

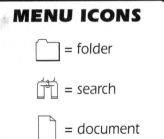

MENU ICONS

📁 = folder

🔍 = search

📄 = document

"Wow," says Zack. "Fun and games looks interesting."

"We'll try that later," answers Kate. "Let's just do one thing at a time." She moves her cursor down the row of folders until it is pointing at the one called **Libraries**. She clicks on that folder and gets a new menu on her screen:

- 📁 **University of Minnesota Libraries**
- 📁 **Electronic Books**
- 📁 **Electronic Journal Collections from CICnet**
- 📁 **Government Information**
- 📁 **Library Catalogs via Telnet**
- 📁 **Library Systems in the Twin Cities**
- 📁 **Library of Congress Records**
- 📁 **MINITEX Veronica service**
- 📁 **Newspapers, Magazines, and Newsletters**
- 📁 **Reference Works**

Again Kate moves her cursor down the list of folders. This time she stops when she is pointing to **Electronic Books**. She clicks on her mouse button and another menu appears:

By Author
By Call Letter
By Title
Search Electronic Books

This time she moves down to the folder next to **By Title** and clicks again. Now the menu is a long list of book titles:

Search Electronic Books
1990 USA Census Information
Aesop's Fables
Aladdin and the Wonderful Lamp
Alice's Adventures in Wonderland
CIA World Factbook 1991
Clinton's Inaugural Address
Complete Works of Shakespeare

Kate scrolls down the list until she reaches:

Moby Dick

By clicking on that folder she gets to page icons which will display the text of *Moby Dick* on her screen. She can save the whole text and then read it later, or even print out the pages of the novel.

"Wow," Zack says. "Surfing the Net is going to be fun."

At that moment, CyberSarge appears on their screen. He is smiling. "Good work, kids. You've learned a lot."

"Thanks," Kate replies. "We couldn't have done it without you."

PART II

Explorer:
Living in Cyberspace

CyberSarge looks at Kate and Zack after they return from their tour of the Internet. From the look on their guide's face, the kids can tell that they did a really good job for their first time out. They are feeling pretty proud, and ready to try again as soon as possible!

"Your training phase is nearly over," he informs them. At the moment he says this, a fully animated cartoon band starts playing on the screen. The players, dressed in wild, cartoony outfits with oversized hats and huge sunglasses are seriously jamming on their instruments. The song they are playing is full of trumpets. This is clearly CyberSarge's way of congratulating the two kids.

Kate and Zack smile at the screen. They are feeling pretty proud of themselves, too.

When the band finishes playing, CyberSarge says, "Now you're ready to pilot your own computer on solo missions into the Internet. Pretty soon you won't need me anymore."

Kate and Zack look at each other. They are proud and happy—and just a little bit scared. But they feel confident that with the help of their pilot's manual and all of the built-in helping devices on the Internet, they will have even more fun the second time. Just as they are about to high-five each other, CyberSarge pops up again on the screen.

"Even though you two have come a long way in your training," CyberSarge informs them, "there is still a little more to learn. Read on, Cadets. You're almost there!"

Chapter 5
The Top Ten Rules for Surfing the Net

Before they can be graduated from Cyberspace Academy, Kate and Zack need to learn the ten basic rules of being online. CyberSarge posts a note about these rules on the computer for Kate and Zack:

File	Edit	View

SURFERS' RULES

The Internet is such a huge and new place, it's easy to get lost in it. It's also easy to forget to use common sense while navigating in cyberspace. Our parents have told us since we were little not to talk to strangers. Well, here we are in a universe of strangers, chatting away. It seems so harmless. But that's not always so.

We often know from unhappy experiences on the school playground not to pick fights with people. Yet there are people who pick fights on the Internet. These fight-pickers are called **flamers**, and picking a fight is called **flaming**.

FLAMING

Flaming is using words to stomp on someone in cyberspace for saying something you consider wrong or just plain stupid, without being reasonable. It's kind of like slamming the door when you're mad. It's not very nice, either. Don't do it.

CYBERSARGE SAYS:

Remember that you are in control when you are online, and you can always log off if someone is giving you a hard time.

In general, cyberspace is kind of like an unsupervised playground. And just like in the offline playground world where there are bullies, it's the same way on the Internet. There are a few nasties lurking in cyberspace who are ready to take advantage of someone if they can.

So how do we deal with them?

Well, just like at home or at school, the Internet has rules to obey in order to keep us out of trouble.

They aren't necessarily written down in a special list. But you'll learn them fast enough as you surf the Net. They have come about because there are an awful lot of people on the Internet and we all need to live together peacefully in cyberspace.

Most of the rules for using the Internet involve the same common sense and common courtesy you use offline.

Here's CyberSarge's list of top ten rules for the Internet:

1. NEVER GIVE OUT PERSONAL INFORMATION.

While online don't tell anyone anything that you wouldn't tell a stranger. It's OK to say, "I'm a brunette with brown eyes and I'm tall." But it's **not** OK to give out your phone number, your address, or your password, or to tell someone when your family is going on vacation.

This means that even while chatting with a newfound friend, sending e-mail, or posting messages, **you have to be careful.** Even if you know you may be able to trust the person you're chatting with, there may be others who are reading your e-mail.

2. AVOID UNPLEASANT SITUATIONS.

Sometimes people feel like they can hide behind the safety of their computer and be rude and nasty to others. It's often tempting to be nasty right back. **Don't!**

You are not required to answer rude or unasked-for messages. Ignoring them is the best way to make them stop. If you get hassled online, tell the sysop of the forum about it. Some mail-reading software has a "twit" filter which can be activated to eliminate messages from users that you have already had bad experiences with. Use the twit filter whenever necessary.

3. ALWAYS BE YOURSELF.

Just as some people hide behind their computers so they can be rude, you might want to pretend you're somebody else. It's natural to want to impress others with how cool we are. Maybe you'd like other people to believe you are older, or even pretend to be a girl instead of a boy.

It's easy to make up stuff when others can't see us. But trying to fool other people not only keeps others from finding out about us, it prevents us from seeing them as they really are. Playing fair online means saying, "I'm being real. I hope you are, too."

4. MAKE A BUDGET AND STICK TO IT.

There are two things to always keep in mind:

A: Being online costs money.

Make a budget you can live with, get it approved by your parents—and then stick to it.

B: Being online takes time.

You have a life offline as well as in cyberspace. Make sure you're not overdoing it.

Remembering these two things will help keep you out of trouble. It's easy to get so caught up in reading messages, writing e-mail, and exploring new areas in cyberspace, that you lose track of time. When your parents get the bill for your time at the end of the month, you can bet you will be put back on track in a hurry! It makes no sense to lose your online time for a week or even a month because you went over your allowed time limit by a few hours.

SYSOP

Sysop stands for **SYS**tem **OP**erator and is the person who runs a computer bulletin board. Sysops oversee a bulletin board's traffic, answer questions not found in FAQ files, and generally make sure that everything runs as smoothly as possible.

FORUM

In online services a forum is a special place for discussing a certain subject.

TWIT FILTER

This is a filter in an e-mail program that you use to catch letters from someone you don't want to hear from, or to trash junk e-mail.

Just tell yourself to stick to whatever allowed amount of time you agree on with your parents, and keep a clock on your desk with an alarm. Many computers even have built-in alarms that you can program to go off when you want them to. Check your computer's manual to see if you have one and how to use it. You might even want to keep a monthly log of time used so that you don't go over your limit.

Have a plan for what you're going to do before you go online. It will save you a lot of time. Some e-mail and newsreader programs let you download messages and articles onto your computer's hard drive. Afterward, when you're offline, you can read and respond to them. That doesn't use up your online time, and it saves money.

5. EXPRESS YOURSELF, BUT STAY COOL.

It doesn't take too long to discover that there are people whose only purpose in posting messages seems to be to insult or put somebody down.

It's OK to complain about stuff you don't like or to have a disagreement with a fellow Internaut. But don't let it get insulting and personal. As you learned, that's called **flaming**, and it's no fun to get flamed. So don't **you** become a flamer!

6. IT'S OK TO BE A NEWBIE.

The Internet is so big and so complicated that it can be very confusing to the newcomer. It takes time to figure out how to reply to a message, engage in a chat, or just find your way around. Remember everybody now on the Net was once a newbie. If you're a newbie, someone on the Net will help you as well. No question is "dumb" if you don't know the answer.

7. USE YOUR COMMON SENSE.

One of the best things about being online is that you can ask a question on almost any topic and you'll be sure to get five answers within an hour of posting your question. The problem is, three of the answers are likely to be wrong. This is not to say that you can't get help, just that you have to judge the quality of the help you get. Everybody has an answer, but not everyone always knows what they are talking about. You have to sort through the information to figure out what is true, what is valuable, and what is right for you. Your experience isn't the same as other people's; their answers aren't necessarily the right ones for you. If something sounds outrageous, it probably is.

8. ONLINE PEOPLE ARE REAL PEOPLE.

If you say something mean or hurtful to someone in real life, you can expect them to react to it, just as you would if someone said something nasty to you. Remember that there is a person behind that remote keyboard, even if you can't see him or her. It's easy to flame and to say things we'd never say face-to-face. That is always a mistake.

9. SHARE IDEAS, SHARE FILES, AND SHARE YOURSELF.

The online world is full of people who are eager to share their information, time, and energy with others. Are you looking for information on recent wheat harvests in the Ukraine, or are you having a computer problem you can't solve? Then post a message. Somebody will tell you the FTP site where you can find the information. Do you need a utility program to keep track of your disk space? Some computer whiz in the online community has probably written one that's free for the asking.

There is a lot of freeware out there for the taking. And if you do find a program that's particularly useful, it's nice to drop an e-mail note to the person who wrote it saying how helpful their program is.

UTILITY PROGRAMS

These are special little programs to help you keep your computer running the way you want it to. Think of these programs like the tools in your parents' toolbox; you may not use those tools all the time, but when something needs fixing in a hurry, you sure are glad to have them!

FREEWARE

Freeware is software that you use and give to your friends without paying for it—and it's OK to do so.

Most important of all: **you** have ideas or information to share as well. Don't be shy! Share! Maybe you just saw a great movie and think other people ought to see it. Post a message about it. This free sharing of information and opinion is what makes the cyberspace universe such a great place to be.

10. CYBERSPACE CAN BE WHATEVER YOU WANT IT TO BE.

This doesn't mean you can ignore what the other Internauts are doing. Remember that we're all navigating through cyberspace together. But it does mean that you have to take part in making the Internet the kind of place you want to hang out in.

If you don't find a newsgroup that covers an area you're interested in, suggest a new one! If you think your school should have a World Wide Web page, as so many schools already do, talk to your teacher, and offer to help create one for your school.

Finally, remember that the Internet is like no other place in the known universe. It's a place that's being created as we go. There are plenty of things for kids to do here, and you can contribute. Think of it as your ticket to the 21st century—even **your** children probably won't have an opportunity to be in on something as new and as free as the Internet can be!

CyberSarge pops up again. "Did you get all that?"
"Yes, sir!" say Zack and Kate.

"OK, we'll continue tomorrow. It's been a long day," says CyberSarge.

Kate and Zack can hardly wait. Tomorrow is the day they'll be graduated from Cyberspace Academy. If you have been paying attention, learning and having fun with them, you'll be ready, too!

Chapter 6
Keeping Your Internet Log:
Plus 12 Logs to Get You Started!

The next morning Zack and Kate hurry into the room and switch on the computer. They wriggle anxiously in their seats. This is their big day. Today they'll be graduated from Cyberspace Academy! They're going to advance from being Cadets to becoming full-fledged Internauts!

"All right, kids, sit up straight," says CyberSarge. "This is the moment you've been waiting for. Are you sure you're ready?"

"We're ready!" Zack and Kate reply in unison, sitting up straighter in their chairs.

CyberSarge begins the Cyberspace Academy oath: "Kate and Zack, do you swear to obey the Top Ten Rules of Surfing the Net which you learned, and to treat your fellow Internauts as you want to be treated?"

"We do!" reply the kids.

"Do you promise not to spend more than the agreed-upon time in cyberspace each week, no matter how much fun you're having?" CyberSarge raises an eyebrow.

Oooh, that is a tough one. But they know the right answer to that question. "We promise."

CyberSarge stands straight and tall as he continues: "You both have completed all the requirements for promotion from Cadets to Internauts. And you have demonstrated the responsibility required of Internet voyagers. Therefore, by the authority vested in me as First Sergeant Abraham Lincoln Kennedy of Cyberspace Academy, I hereby pronounce you, Kate, and you, Zack—full-fledged Internauts!"

"Yahoo! Way cool!" Zack and Kate shout—causing their mother downstairs to call up: "Is everything OK?"

"We're fine, Mom," Kate replies, grinning at her brother.

They turn back to the screen—and it is blank! CyberSarge is gone!

"CyberSarge! Where are you?" Zack calls, tapping the enter key on the keyboard.

"I'm still here," CyberSarge's voice comes from the computer. "But I won't be much longer. You two are ready to travel through cyberspace on your own. My voice will come up in any real emergency, but I'm confident there won't be any more of those. You two have been excellent students."

"You can't leave!" Zack cries. "What if we need you, CyberSarge?"

"You know all you need to know about traveling the Internet," CyberSarge replies. "You have this book to refer to in case you forget anything, not to

mention the Glossary and the Index of Terms if you
need a reminder about any of the terms we've
discussed. Besides, I've got more Cadets to train."

"How do we know where to go? Or how to get
there?" Kate asks. "What if we get lost?"

"You have more help than you could possibly
need," replies CyberSarge. "The Internet is filled with
folks who love to help. Why, I'll bet that before long,
you'll be the ones answering questions from some
newbies!"

CyberSarge appears again one last time and salutes
them. "Congratulations, Zack and Kate. You have
done well. Goodbye."

Kate and Zack are surprised and a little bit
nervous as they salute back. "Well, see ya,
CyberSarge," Zack says, sounding a little unsure.
"Thanks again for everything!" he remembers to add.

"What do we do now?" Kate asks.

On the screen, CyberSarge begins to
fade from view. His voice gets softer as
he says, "In the next section of this
guide, I've included a list of places to
start exploring. And don't forget to keep
a log in the spaces provided of where
you've been so if you ever want to get
back there, you'll be able to find the
places in cyberspace easily. You'll get a
few more screen messages from me
throughout this book, but from now on,
you're on your own!" CyberSarge is gone.
In his place a message scrolls across the screen.

File   Edit   View

YOUR INTERNET LOG

It's a good idea to keep track of where you've been on the Internet. Even if you write down the address, you may forget what you found there. Here's a system, which is borrowed from the old newspaper reporter's rule book:

Who: This is the name of the site.

How: This is how you got there: Web, Gopher, FTP, Usenet, Telnet, IRC, e-mail list, etc.

Where: This is the address. Be careful to spell it correctly and use capital or lowercase letters when needed.

What: Write down a brief description of what the place is all about. Don't make it too long, but be sure to put in enough information so you remember what it was like.

Why: These are the reasons you would want to go back there again, or maybe why you wouldn't.

When: If this is a very busy place, you might want to write down whether it's best to call in the morning or on weekends, or whenever there might be less online traffic.

We provide you here with several pages of charts for you to use for logging. When you run out of space, just set up a notebook and create your own new Internet log. As Kate and Zack have already learned in Cyberspace Academy, once you take your first ride in cyberspace, you'll be cruising to new places all the time!

_____'S INTERNET SURFER'S LOG

WHO _____

HOW _____

WHERE _____

WHAT _____

_____

_____

_____

WHY _____

_____

_____

WHEN _____

_____

_____

_____

_____'S INTERNET SURFER'S LOG

WHO _____

HOW _____

WHERE _____

WHAT _____

_____

_____

WHY _____

_____

_____

WHEN _____

_____

_____

_____'S INTERNET SURFER'S LOG

WHO _____

HOW _____

WHERE _____

WHAT_____

_____

_____

WHY _____

_____

_____

WHEN _____

_____

_____

_____'S INTERNET SURFER'S LOG

WHO _____

HOW _____

WHERE _____

WHAT_____

_____

_____

WHY _____

_____

_____

WHEN _____

_____

_____

_____'S INTERNET SURFER'S LOG

WHO _____

HOW _____

WHERE _____

WHAT_____

_____

_____

WHY _____

_____

_____

WHEN _____

_____

_____

_____'S INTERNET SURFER'S LOG

WHO _____

HOW _____

WHERE _____

WHAT_____

_____

_____

WHY _____

_____

_____

WHEN _____

_____

_____

_____'S INTERNET SURFER'S LOG

WHO _____

HOW _____

WHERE _____

WHAT _____

_____

_____

_____

WHY _____

_____

_____

WHEN _____

_____

_____

_____

_____'S INTERNET SURFER'S LOG

WHO _____

HOW _____

WHERE _____

WHAT _____

_____

_____

WHY _____

_____

_____

WHEN _____

_____

_____'S INTERNET SURFER'S LOG

WHO _____

HOW _____

WHERE _____

WHAT_____

_____

_____

WHY _____

_____

_____

WHEN _____

_____

_____

_____'S INTERNET SURFER'S LOG

WHO _____

HOW _____

WHERE _____

WHAT_____

_____

_____

WHY _____

_____

_____

WHEN _____

_____

_____

_____'S INTERNET SURFER'S LOG

WHO _____

HOW _____

WHERE _____

WHAT_____

_____

_____

WHY _____

_____

_____

WHEN _____

_____

_____

_____'S INTERNET SURFER'S LOG

WHO _____

HOW _____

WHERE _____

WHAT_____

_____

_____

WHY _____

_____

_____

WHEN _____

_____

_____

Chapter 7
Guide to the Galaxy:
Cool Places to Surf on the Net

Kate and Zack are online and
ready to surf the Net. Now so
are you! CyberSarge has one
last message to share with you
about the cool places you
might want to visit.

File	Edit	View

MESSAGE FROM CYBERSARGE
TO ALL INTERNAUTS

All right, Internauts, you've learned the ins and outs of
your spacecraft, traveled to a few places, talked with
people from all over the world—all with CyberSarge as
your guide.

Now it's time for you to pilot all of your solo voyages
into the vast reaches of the Internet. You won't need a
map. Cyberspace is changing too rapidly to provide an
up-to-date map anyway.

What you will need is a way to find the places you're
looking for. A rough rule of thumb for travelers is: If
you're looking for graphical sites—sites that have pictures
or links to other places, pictures, and movies—start with

GRAPHICAL SITES

These are places in cyberspace
that have pictures or links to
other places, pictures, and
movies. The World Wide Web is
one of the best places to find
graphical sites.

CYBERSARGE'S GALACTIC HOTSPOTS

1. STARTING POINTS

How to get where you need to go.

2. PEOPLE & PLACES

All around the world. Includes a list of IRCs.

3. SCIENCE & MATH

From bees to NASA space shuttles.

4. HISTORY

Journey through the past.

5. READING & WRITING

From sci-fi to the classics.

6. ART & MUSIC

Painting, sculpture, photography , artists and pop stars.

7. CURRENT AFFAIRS

All the news, far and wide.

8. COMPUTERS

Helpful advice, new software, and solutions to common problems.

9. FUN & GAMES

Everything from kites to World Conquest.

10. SPORTS

All leagues all the time.

11. ENTERTAINMENT

Welcome to the world of show biz.

12. LIBRARIES

Reference material on any and all subjects.

13. USENET NEWSGROUPS FOR KIDS

Over 50 kid-friendly newsgroups.

the World Wide Web. The Web is the fastest growing part of the Internet.

If you're looking for files, games, or useful computer utilities, FTP sites is where you'll find them.

Usenet newsgroups—from **alt.1d**, which discusses one-dimensional thinking; to **wi.transit**, which talks about what's happening in Wisconsin—all provide places for discussions. For instance, **news.answers** provides useful news information. You'll find discussions that are interesting, fun, or just plain strange on just about any topic you can think of, not to mention the many topics you can't imagine—until you happen to land there!

Other areas in which to chat about your favorite topics or to lurk and read what others have to say are mailing lists.

To get you started, here's a list of galactic hotspots.

These are some cool places that you may want to check out while traveling through the Internet.

There are, as of this message, almost 40,000 active Web sites on the Internet. There are over 10,000 active newsgroups, both national and local. There are thousands of mailing lists, Gopher sites, and remote computer locations you can FTP or Telnet to. Whatever you're looking for, you'll probably find it on the Internet.

Some of the places you pick to visit might not be there anymore. But that's OK. With so many new sites going online each day, you're sure to find something else that's just as interesting. The places on this list have been around for quite a while and almost certainly will be there when you log on to them.

Here's an important thing to remember: You don't have to travel in cyberspace like you do in real space, going first to A, then to B, and so on. You can jump from A to Z just as quickly!

Ready? Here we go!

This list is divided into 13 useful sections.

1. STARTING POINTS

These are some selected home pages that are jumping off points to begin your voyages onto the Internet.

Who: YAHOO
How: Web
Where: *http://www.yahoo.com*
What: Yahoo is one of the best known search start points on the World Wide Web. Yahoo was started as a hobby by two Stanford University students, and has since become one of the most useful and popular jumping off points on the Net. This online guide to the Internet has simplified life for hundreds of thousands of Internet users. There is a simple menu that lets you search for items by category, or you can do a key word search if you know what subject you're looking for. Even if you're just browsing this is perhaps the best place on the Web to start looking.

Who: KIDS ON THE WEB
How: Web
Where: *http://www.zen.org:80/brendan/kids. html*
What: This is an ongoing list of sites that offers information for and about kids. Among other things, it includes a lot of stuff to play with, and some information about education and schools from kindergarten to high school. This list offers a body of information that people can use either to

CYBERSARGE SAYS AGAIN:

When you see an address that takes up more than one line in this book, such as:

http://www.state.com/
city/street.html

it should be typed out on one line with no spaces where the line breaks. Remember there are never any spaces in Internet addresses.

let their kids play with stuff on the Internet, or to find the things they need for their work related to the care and education of children.

Who: THE VIRTUAL LIBRARY
How: Web
Where: *http://info.cern.ch/hypertext/ DataSources/bySubject/Overview.html*
What: This page is the home of the World Wide Web's Virtual Library at the University of Bern in Switzerland. CERN, the European Laboratory for Particle Physics, is where the World Wide Web was started. The Virtual Library lists thousands of Web locations, both by subject area and by their geographic location. Want to find a Web site in Kenya? Here's where you can start browsing.

Who: UNCLE BOB'S KIDS PAGE
How: Web
Where: *http://www/gagme.wwa.com:80/~boba/ kids.html*
What: Uncle Bob's Kids Page is a real treasure chest of links, which has been cleaned, checked, and annotated, with spotlights on special subjects of interest to kids of all ages. It's a great place to start your journey through the Net.

Who: GLOBAL NETWORK NAVIGATOR
How: Web
Where: *http://nearnet.gnn.com/gnn.html*
What: This is the address for the Global Network Navigator, which has links to thousands of sites, as well as its own online magazines. There are also search capabilities to help you find the site you've heard about, but don't know the address to get there.

Who: NCSA'S WHAT'S NEW PAGE
How: Web
Where: *http://www.gnn.com/gnn/wn/whats-new.html*
What: This is the unofficial newspaper of the World Wide Web. NCSA (**N**ational **C**enter for **S**upercomputing **A**pplications) What's New Page is the source for the latest Web listings. It's updated a couple of times a week, and is a good place to look for what's new on the Web.

Who: MOSAIC™ HOME PAGE
How: Web
Where: *http://www.ncsa.uiuc.edu/SDG/Software/Mosaic/NCSAMosaicHome.html*
What: This is the Mosaic™ home page. Mosaic™ was the original Web browser program and the model for all other browsers. Not only is it freeware, it's also still one of the best Web browsers around. Mosaic's home page is likewise another good place to begin your Internet travels.

FREENET

These are bulletin board systems that are connected to the Internet and are free of charge. Usually these are sponsored by community groups to give people free access to computing and information.

Who:	USA CITYLINK
How:	Web
Where:	*http://www.NeoSoft.com/citylink*
What:	The USA CityLink project is the most comprehensive United States city and state listing on the Web, as well as one of the most well visited sites on the Internet. It provides users with a starting point when accessing information about U.S. states and cities. State home pages, city pages, CityLink pages, and freenet home pages will be listed here as they are created.

2. PEOPLE & PLACES

These are some interesting places where you can find out about people and places from all around the world.

Who:	VIRTUAL TOWN
How:	Web
Where:	*http://www.cs.ucdavis.edu/virt-town/welcome.html*
What:	Virtual Town is a World Wide Web index in the form of a small town. If you have a graphical browser, like Netscape™, it shows the town as a map, with locations such as "Government Offices," "arcade," "post office," and so on, which are actually links to other pages full of links to other Web sites. Be aware that the graphical town image might take five minutes to load into your computer. It's worth a look, but if you use Virtual Town a lot, you can get around a lot faster with

GRAPHICAL BROWSER

A graphical browser is a browsing program that allows you to search for documents and sites with pictures in them.

the text-based map, which is located at the URL address: ***http://www.cs.ucdavis. edu/virt-town/town-txt.html***

Who: THE INTERNATIONAL ARCTIC
       PROJECT
How: Web
Where: ***http://scholastic.com:2005***
What: In early 1995, veteran explorer, author, and educator Will Steger and his team of six international explorers and scientists began an expedition to the North Pole. They plan to be the first people (that we know about, anyway) to cross the Arctic tundra in a single season. They want to publicize their mission in order to make people more aware of the global importance of the Arctic. The International Arctic Project will be live online and on the Internet at Scholastic. This site can also be reached by Gopher at: ***scholastic.com***. (Be sure to reset the Gopher port from the standard 70 to 2003.) The International Arctic Project Home Page offers lots of information on the explorers, their route, the dog sled teams, what they're eating, and more. There will be updates, photos, and reports throughout the year.

Who: SUBWAY NAVIGATOR
How: Gopher
Where: *gopher.jussieu.fr/11/metro/*
What :   This site lets you check routes on subway systems all over the world. Currently it includes, among other cities: New York, San Francisco, London, Washington, Milan, Paris, Marseille, Toronto, Hong Kong, Tokyo, Montreal, Chicago, and Amsterdam. It not only gives you the route between your starting point and destination, it also gives you the estimated travel time.

    You can also Telnet directly to the site through: *metro.jussieu.fr:10000/*

Who: INTERNET RELAY CHAT
How: IRC
Where: Here are all the addresses for IRCs in the USA. You'll need to check them out to see what each chat is about.
cs-pub.bu.edu
hobbes.catt.ncsu.edu
irc-2.mit.edu
irc.bga.com
irc.colorado.edu
irc.csos.orst.edu
irc.digex.netirc.duq.edu
irc.iastate.edu
irc.eskimo.com
irc.math.byu.edu
irc.math.ufl.edu
irc.uiuc.edu
merlin.acf-lab.alaska.edu

nova.unix.portal.com

organ.ctr.columbia.edu

poe.acc.virginia.edu

sluaxa.slu.edu

IRCs in Canada:

atlantis.cc.mcgill.ca

castor.cc.manitoba.ca

degaulle.hil.ubn.ca

neumann.info.polymtl.ca

IRCs in Germany:

noc.belwue.de

sokrates.informatik.uni-kl.de

uni-karlsruhe.de

uni-stuttgart.de

IRCs in the United Kingdom:

ismayl.demon.co.uk

serv.eng.abdn.ac.uk

shrug.dur.ac.uk

stork.doc.ic.ac.uk

IRCs in Sweden:

gwaihir.dd.chalmers.se

irc.nada.kth.se

krynn.efd.lth.se

In Japan:

bohemia.jaist.ac.jp

hamlet.nff.ncl.omron.co.jp

hemp.imel.kyoto-u.ac.jp

irc.ubec.ac.jp

omrongw.wg.omron.co.jp

scslwide.sony.co.jp

What: These are some IRC sites around the world that you can try out.

3. SCIENCE & MATH

Since the Internet started as a place for teachers and scientists to exchange information, it's natural that there would be thousands of sites devoted to math and the sciences. More and more World Wide Web sites like these are appearing every day.

Who: BEES IN THE WEB
How: Web
Where: *http://gears.tucson.ars.ag.gov*
What: Don't let the long name of the Carl Hayden Bee Research Center's Global Entomology Agricultural Research Server scare you off; this hive of activity brings you everything you want to know about bees in a pleasant, informal atmosphere. Read neat bee facts in the Internet Classroom and Tri*bee*al Pursuits, and learn what to do if you meet an angry swarm of African honey bees. Their sensible advice: *Run*! The site offers scads of images, sound files, and movies (Insect Theater On-Line) of various insects found in Arizona's Sonoran Desert.

Who: KANSAS ASTRONOMY
How: Web
Where: *http://www.twsu.edu/o0.html*
What: This Kansas site is yet another Web destination bringing outer space to cyberspace. Astronomical images from the Hubble telescope and the observatory's own CCD camera (Charged Coupled Device or a sensor for a video camera that converts what the camera sees into video

signals) are offered. Some of the images are large but all are stored on site, avoiding the crowds at NASA (NASA is the National Aeronautics and Space Administration)—though you can hop over to NASA and to other astronomy sites via links that they provide. Helpful text files explain some of the images, but if you're still perplexed after reading them, you can always ask one of the astronomers for help. The observatory has other information that might be worth viewing if you plan to visit or are a grade-school teacher looking for astronomy teaching aids.

Who: NASA/JPL IMAGING RADAR HOME PAGE
How: Web
Where: ***http://southport.jpl.nasa.gov***
What: Explore imaging radar and the ways it is used at this home page of the National Aeronautics and Space Administration (NASA) and Jet Propulsion Labs (JPL). View the picture gallery of images, play videos and watch animation, and find out about the space shuttle missions that carried the Spaceborne Radar Laboratory. The science and applications section explains how to obtain radar images of many areas around the globe. Fill out a license agreement, and receive JPL software for reading and analyzing radar data.

Who: JONATHAN'S SPACE REPORT

How: Web

Where: *http://hea-www.harvard.edu/QEDT/ jcm/jsr.html*

What: Jonathan's Space Report is put out by Jonathan McDowell at the Harvard-Smithsonian Center for Astrophysics. It appears about once a week on the Web. The text-based report covers many aspects of space vehicle launches and returns from all over our planet. The report is also available for downloading by FTP at: *ftp:// saoftp.harvard.edu/pub/jcm/space/news*

Who: NASA

How: Web

Where: *http://mosaic.larc.nasa.gov/nasaonline/ nasaonline.html*

What: This is your direct gateway to NASA, the National Aeronautics and Space Administration, where you can find out everything you ever wanted to know about our space program. You can even take a virtual voyage into outer space!

Who: EXPLORATORIUM

How: Web

Where: *http://www.exploratorium.edu*

What: San Francisco's famous Exploratorium Museum is much more than just a museum. It's a total educational center with a collection of interactive exhibits in science, art, nature, and technology. This site is highly recommended by the editors of this book as a great place to visit.

Who: THE MEDICAL ILLUSTRATORS'
HOME PAGE

How: Web

Where: *http://siesta.packet.net/med_illustrator/*
Welcome.html

What: Some of us never got past dissecting frogs.
That was gross enough. But for those in
the medical and publishing fields, the
Medical Illustrators' Home Page gives an
excellent preview of a variety of
illustrations of the anatomy and other
subjects from some very talented artists.
Links to related sites are also available.

Who: MUSEUM OF PALEONTOLOGY

How: Web

Where: *http://ucmp1.berkeley.edu/exhibittext/*
entrance.html

What: Like dinosaurs? You'll love this cybertour
of the famous collection of dinosaur
bones and dinosaur lore at the University
of California at Berkeley.

Who: SPACELINK

How: Telnet

Where: *spacelink.msfc.nasa.gov*

What: In addition to being a great place to
explore, you can ask a scientist outer
space-related questions and get an e-mail
reply, usually within a day or two.
Because this is such a popular site, it may
take you a while to log on.

Who: MATH PROBLEMS AND PUZZLES
How: FTP
Where: *ftp.csd.uwm.edu/pub*
What: This is an FTP site filled with math problems and puzzles. It's a good place to find the answers to those tough math homework questions, or the solutions to math puzzles. It's a place where math can be fun.

4. HISTORY

These sites are great places to go digging for historical information. Here are some great places for learning about the past.

Who: MUSEUM OF PHOTOGRAPHY
How: Web
Where: *http://cmp1.ucr.edu*
What: The University of California at Riverside has a Museum of Photography with many historical pictures, as well as art and kids' projects.

Who: LIBRARY OF CONGRESS
How: Telnet
Where: *locis.loc.gov*
What: Here's the granddaddy of all libraries. It's the ultimate database for doing your history research—or any kind of research. You can also reach the Library of Congress by Gopher at: *marvel.loc.gov*

Who: AMERICAN MEMORY
How: Web
Where: *http://rs6.loc.gov/amhome.html*
What: This is a special collection from the Library of Congress. If you think history is boring, think again! Drop in here and take a fascinating journey back in American history.

5. READING & WRITING

From great classics of literature to today's popular novels, these are places to visit if you love to read.

Who: THE CHILDREN'S LITERATURE HOME PAGE
How: Web
Where: *http://www.ucalgary.ca/~dkbrown/index. html*
What: This is a great guide to children's literature resources on the Internet. It includes awards lists from Canada, the U.S., and beyond, and lists of recommended reading such as the "Recommended Books for the Reluctant Young Reader," list from the American Library Association Gopher. Other links lead to information about authors and fictional characters, electronic children's books, children's literature discussion groups, and resources for parents and teachers.

Who: SCIENCE FICTION LOVERS
How: FTP
Where: *elbereth.rutgers.edu/pub/sfl*
What: This is a huge collection of text files from various Usenet newsgroups dealing with science fiction and fantasy. There's information and FAQs on just about everything sci-fi, from alternate histories to an episode guide for your favorite TV series.

Who: BABEL
How: E-mail
Where: *listserv@vm.temple.edu*
What: The latest issue of "BABEL: A Glossary of Computer-Oriented Abbreviations and Acronyms" is available through e-mail. To subscribe, send a message to: *listserv@vm.temple.edu* In the body of the message type: *GET BABEL95A TXT*

6. ART & MUSIC

Pictures and songs, great artists and musicians, pop and rock stars—they all hang out here.

Who: LE LOUVRE
How: Web
Where: *http://mistral.enst.fr/~pioch/louvre/*
What: One of the most famous art museums in the world, France's Le Louvre is now online as a virtual museum in cyberspace. There are paintings by Van Gogh, Cezanne, and other master artists including Leonardo da Vinci's masterpiece "Mona Lisa." There are usually one or two special exhibits

available for viewing as well. This is a visual feast for any art lover.

Who: RYDER'S AMERICAN ART
      MUSEUM GOPHER
How: Gopher
Where: *ryder.si.edu*
What: Ryder is the Internet server maintained by the National Museum of American Art, the Smithsonian Institution, to provide public access to museum research and educational materials including the museum's calendar of events, hours, and exhibitions. The server also contains images and multimedia software. Images are accessible by category, artist, and title. Online visitors interested in multimedia are provided access to image-viewing software and interactives that can be downloaded. The museum shop is also online with various museum products such as publications, curriculum packets, gifts, and subscriptions.

7. CURRENT AFFAIRS

Find out what's happening in your neighborhood and the rest of the world through Internet newspapers.

Who: THE WHITE HOUSE
How: Web
Where: *http://www.whitehouse.gov*
What: Take a virtual visit to the President's house. You can even leave an e-mail message to tell them how much you enjoyed the tour.

Who: THE ELECTRONIC TELEGRAPH
How: Web
Where: *http://www.telegraph.co.uk*
What: Great Britain's first electronic newspaper is *The Electronic Telegraph* (based on the *London Daily Telegraph*), with news of the world that you sometimes can't find in the United States, as well as some tough crossword puzzles. When you register with the Electronic Telegraph to receive your news online, you will receive a PIN that you have to remember the next time. As with all passwords and numbers you'll need, write them down somewhere (perhaps in your Internet Log), and don't tell anyone what they are.

Who: SAN JOSE MERCURY
How: Web
Where: *http://www.sjmercury.com*
What: The online edition of the *San Jose Mercury*, is located in Northern California's Silicon Valley, which is the home of many major computer hardware and software companies, including Hewlett-Packard and Apple Computers.

Who: TIME
How: Web
Where: *http://www.timeinc.com/time/universe. html*
What: *Time* magazine has a jam-packed World Wide Web page with photos and articles from their current issues, back issue archives, and lots more.

PIN

PIN stands for **P**ersonal **I**dentification **N**umber and is used for cards for automated bank machines to make sure the person using the card owns the card. They are personal passwords that allow you to use the card to withdraw money or perform other services.

8. COMPUTERS

Got a computer problem? Confused by something new on the Internet? You'll find helpful advice here.

Who: IBM™
How: Web
Where: *http://www.ibm.com*
What: This is the home page for all things IBM™, from software to hardware.

Who: APPLE SUPPORT SERVICE
How: FTP
Where: *ftp.apple.com*
What: Basically this is a storage area for Apple-related software, going back to System 5. (Apple is the company that makes Macintosh™ computers, among others.) Because most of the files are really large, you'd better have a very fast modem before you decide to download from here—or you'll be sitting around waiting for quite a while.

Who: MICROSOFT HOME PAGE
How: Web
Where: *http://www/microsoft.com*
What: For the latest on Windows™ or anything else that Microsoft is doing, this the place to start. There's a lot of the latest information on their products, plus updates and support files for downloading. You can FTP to the file area through: *ftp.microsoft.com*

9. FUN & GAMES

Want to play a game or just hang out? These are the places to be.

Who: THE KITE ORACLE
How: Usenet
Where: *rec.kites*
What: The wind in your face, a kite string in your hand—this is happiness to the members of this newsgroup. They take the subject of kites very seriously indeed! Want to find a good, two-line kite that packs up small enough to put in a carry-on bag? Or what's a good kite catalog? The threads from one kite-related topic to another can get pretty technical, but you can also find out about the 1995 New Zealand Kite Festival and perhaps join online interactive lectures and workshops with international kite experts. You can find archives of previous messages and other files via FTP at: *ftp.hawaii.edu/pub/rec/kites*

Who: SEGA
How: Web
Where: *http://www.sega.com*
What: Sega, the game manufacturer, has its own Web site. Here you can find the latest updates on their catalog and price lists with lots of graphics.

Who: WORLD CONQUEST
How: Web
Where: *http://dnai.com/~conquest*
What: This is the site of an online multiplayer
        strategy game called World Conquest.

10. SPORTS

Here's where to go for sports in general or to follow
the status of your favorite team.

Who: MINOR LEAGUE SPORTS
How: Web
Where: *http://www.deltanet.com/minorleagues*
What: Are you a fan of minor league sports?
        Here's a World Wide Web site with
        information, teams, stats, and other great
        stuff about minor league baseball, hockey,
        and Arena football.

Who: ESPN SPORTS
How: Web
Where: *http://espnet.sportszone.com*
What: Welcome to The ESPN Studios. Get up-
        to-the-minute program updates and TV
        listings here. Find out what's going on
        inside ESPN, ESPN2, and ESPN Radio.
        You can download photos and learn more
        about your favorite ESPN personalities.
        Then for the latest sports news,
        information, and lots of other cool stuff,
        you can head back to the front page of the
        ESPNET SportsZone.

11. ENTERTAINMENT

These are places to find out about movies, TV, and what's happening in the world of showbiz and theater.

Who: X-FILES
How: Web
Where: *http://www.rutgers.edu/x-files.html*
What: This is the *X-Files* TV show home page which has links to lots of *X-Files* FAQs and other sites. Play the theme music, listen to the fall season promo, scan the episode guide, and read what *X-Files* fans have to say about the episodes.

Who: ANIMANAICS
How: Web
Where: *http://www2.msstate.edu/~jbp3/animx/animx.html*
What: This is the *Animaniacs* TV cartoon home page. It's not quite as involved as the *X-Files* page, but it has the **alt.tv.animaniacs.** New Reader's Guide— a must-read "Quick Start" list of services and references available. Also contains helpful netiquette hints.

Who: CYBERWALK
How: Web
Where: *http://www.mca.com*
What: MCA/Universal City Studios provides a home page on the World Wide Web about all their TV shows and movies. The Universal Channel has cartoons and live-action clips to download including full-

length previews of upcoming movies and photographs of various celebrities. Surf on over for a look at an episode guide from the TV show *Exosquad*, as well as a movie guide to recent and upcoming films. There is also lots of information about the music divisions which includes upcoming concerts, and merchandise such as T-shirts and CDs. This is also the jumping off point for other MCA sites including The Putnam Berkley Group, which is the parent company of Price Stern Sloan, the publishers of this book! The Putnam Berkley Group offers a list of books available at:

http://www.putnam.com

Who: PARAMOUNT PICTURES
How: Web
Where: *http://paramount.com*
What: This is the home page of Paramount Pictures with information on their TV shows and movies, including a *Star Trek: Voyager* home page.

Who: SONY
How: Web
Where: *http://music.sony.com*
What: This is where you can find all sorts of information on Sony recording artists, their concerts, music and video clips, movies, and more.

Who: KABUKI FOR EVERYONE
How: Web
Where: *http://www.fix.co.jp/kabuki.html*
What: This is a home page which introduces the traditional form of Japanese theater to the world. It includes pictures, sounds, and downloadable videos. It is also an example of a home page that has foreign language pages in addition to the basic English versions.

12. LIBRARIES

Here's where you can find reference material on any subject.

Who: THE INTERNET PUBLIC LIBRARY
How: Web
Where: *http://ipl.sils.umich.edu*
What: In the Youth Division, young people can Ask the Author questions about his or her life and writing—really famous children's books authors appear here! You can also discuss books with Bookie the bookworm, attend a Story Hour, enter a Writing Contest, and more.

Who: ALEX
How: Gopher
Where: *gopher://gopher.lib.ncsu.edu/11/library/stacks/Alex*
What: ALEX is a catalogue of electronic texts on the Internet. It's a library of over 1800 online books that can be searched by author, title, or subject.

Who: NEWS ANSWERS
How: Usenet
Where: ***news.answers***
What: This Usenet newsgroup is a collection of
       FAQs on other newsgroups and general
       Internet information. It's probably one of
       the newsgroups you'll want to subscribe
       to, at least when you're still feeling your
       way around the Net. You might also want
       to look at: ***news.announce.newusers***

Who: ENCYCLOPEDIA BRITANNICA
       ONLINE
How: Web
Where: ***http://www.eb.com***
What: Britannica Online is a virtual
       encyclopedia online. It's a commercial
       service, which means you'll have to
       subscribe to be able to access the more
       than 14-million-word–hypertext database.
       But there is a demo area where you can
       get a taste of what it's like, and whether or
       not it's for you.

13. USENET NEWSGROUPS FOR KIDS

Here is a list of Usenet newsgroups that kids will enjoy visiting.To get to Usenets, simply look in the menu of the Internet software provided by your online service company. (This list is long! So we've used the alphabet to separate the entries. When we got to "z" we started again with "aa"—just so you won't get confused.)

Who: USENET NEWSGROUPS FOR KIDS
How: Usenet
Where: Various topics at various sites:

a. About Isaac Asimov, writer:
   alt.books.isaac-asimov

b. About Batman:
   alt.comics.batman

c. About Superman:
   alt.comics.superman

d. Ghost stories on the Net:
   alt.folklore.ghost-stories

e. Information for new users on the Net:
   news.announce.newusers

f. FAQ lists and other periodic postings from various newsgroups:
   news.answers

g. Here's where you can ask questions about Usenet:
   news.newusers.questions

h. For Ren and Stimpy fans:
   alt.fan.ren-and-stimpy

i. Here's a place to trade comic books:
   rec.arts.comics.marketplace

j. For reviews of science fiction:
   rec.arts.sf.reviews

k. Discussions about Warner Bros. cartoons:
   alt.animation.warner-bros

l. Write to the guy in the red suit:
   santa@north.pole.org

m. The first network for kids:
   alt.tv.nickelodeon

n. Discussion about the *Tiny Toon Adventures* show:
   alt.tv.tiny-toon

o. The use of computers by children:
   misc.kids.computer

p. Discussion on all forms of family-oriented vacationing:
   misc.kids.vacation

q. Discussion of various kinds of animation:
   rec.arts.animation

r. All about dwarfish trees and shrubbery:
   rec.arts.bonsai

s. Discussion of any Disney-related subjects:
   rec.arts.disney

t. Discussions of movies and movie-making:
   rec.arts.movies

u. *Babylon 5* creators meet fans here:
   rec.arts.sf.tv.babylon5

v. New *Star Trek* shows, movies, books:
   rec.arts.startrek.current

w. *Star Trek* conventions and memorabilia:
   rec.arts.startrek.fandom

x. General discussions about bicycling:
   rec.bicycles.misc

y. For hobbyists interested in bird watching:
   rec.birds

z. About collecting sports and nonsports cards:
   rec.collecting.cards

NETIQUETTE

This is simply the proper way to behave when you're surfing the Internet, such as respecting the rights and opinions of others, and treating others the way you want to be treated.

aa. Folk dances, dancers, dancing:
rec.folk-dancing

bb. Food, cooking, cookbooks, recipes:
rec.food.cooking

cc. Chess and computer chess:
rec.games.chess

dd. Discussion of Chinese chess, Xiangqi:
rec.games.chinese-chess

ee. Announcements of happenings in the role-playing world:
rec.games.frp.announce

ff. All about Nintendo video game systems and software:
rec.games.video.nintendo

gg. All about Sega video game systems and software:
rec.games.video.sega

hh. Juggling techniques, equipment, events:
rec.juggling

ii. Model railroads of all scales:
rec.models.railroad

jj. Radio-controlled models for hobbyists:
rec.models.rc

kk. Country & western music, performers, concerts:
rec.music.country.western

ll. Pets, pet care, household animals:
rec.pets

mm. The culture and care of indoor birds:
rec.pets.birds

nn. Discussion about domestic cats:
rec.pets.cats

oo. Any and all subjects relating to dogs as pets:
rec.pets.dogs

pp. Reptiles, amphibians, other exotic
vivarium pets:
rec.pets.herp

qq. Puzzles, problems, quizzes:
rec.puzzles

rr. Scouting your organizations worldwide:
rec.scouting

ss. Ice skating and roller skating:
rec.skate

tt. Discussion about baseball:
rec.sport.baseball

uu. Astronomy discussions and information:
sci.astro

vv. Biology and related sciences:
sci.bio

ww. Chemistry and related sciences:
sci.chem

xx. Discussion of solid earth sciences:
sci.geo.geology

yy. Mathematical discussions and pursuits:
sci.math

zz. Physical laws, properties, etc.:
sci.physics

aaa. Announcements of space-related news
items:
sci.space.news

bbb. About the space shuttle:
sci.space.shuttle

ccc. Virtual reality technology and culture:
sci.virtual-worlds

ddd. Announcements/requests about people
on the Net:
sci.net-people

eee. In search of Net friendships?:
soc.penpals

fff. A place for the pre-college set on the Net:
alt.kids-talk

ggg. Wildlife related discussions and information:
rec.animals.wildlife

What: Cool Usenet newsgroups for kids.

PART III

Commander:

Welcome Parents and Teachers

O:-)   <:-)   :-)   (:-)   :-o   :-!   :-D   :-p   (:-&   :-"   :-\

On page 45 CyberSarge appears on the computer screen and asks Kate and Zack to bring in their parents or their teacher so they can share in their children's new experience on the Internet.

In the following chapters, CyberSarge provides information for both kids and their grown-ups. Chapter 8 will give you information about choosing an online company or service provider; and Chapter 9 provides logs where you can record your Internet provider information.

Chapter 10 is specifically for grown-ups. It discusses issues that will help guide adults in this fascinating adventure through the new world their kids have come to know as cyberspace. Once the adult has read this information, he or she can use the Official Internet Contract which both adult and child can amend, agree to, and then sign.

Chapter 8

Finding Your Cybership:

Choosing an Online Company or Service Provider

This is CyberSarge's list and comments on some national online services and Internet gateway providers. In addition to these national services, there will be several local providers in your city, state, or region that you can also use to access the Internet.

If you don't already have a gateway provider this list is a good place to start.

THERE ARE THREE BASIC WAYS TO GET ON THE INTERNET:

1. **YOU CAN JOIN A COMMERCIAL ONLINE SERVICE**, such as CompuServe, America Online, Delphi, eWorld, or Prodigy. Beginning in 1995, these services are all offering full Internet access.

2. **YOU CAN SIGN UP WITH A NATIONAL INTERNET SERVICE PROVIDER** such as PSI's Pipeline™, Netcom's Netcruiser™, or PSI's Interramp™. They do not have all the features of the commercial services, such as access to some of the national news services and magazines, large databases of files for downloading, or special educational and entertainment forums. But they are usually less expensive, and most of the services they do not offer can already be found somewhere on the Internet.

3. **YOU CAN SIGN UP WITH A LOCAL INTERNET PROVIDER IN YOUR AREA**. This is often the least expensive solution, but the setup or installation of the software can be more complicated. You'll usually be using a third-party software package, which they can provide if you don't have your own programs. Like the national providers, local Internet providers do not have all of the features of the commercial online services.

COMMERCIAL ONLINE SERVICES

First let's look at the commercial online services. You or someone you know may already be a member of one of these. You've probably seen their ads in national magazines, on TV, or maybe received their free software in the mail or in an issue of a magazine. They make getting onto the Net really easy. Usually all you have to do is install or set up the software, point the cursor, and click.

The major commercial online services are as follows. All of the following information is correct at the time this book went to press.

AMERICA ONLINE (AOL)

Contact: 800-827-6364

Users: 2 million

Cost: Currently $9.95/month for five hours online; $2.95/each additional hour.

AOL offers free software, has a quick and easy menu system, and provides Internet e-mail, FTP, newsgroups, and mailing lists, but no Telnet or IRC. They offer a World Wide Web browser at no extra cost. AOL also offers material from *Time, U.S. News & World Report, the Chicago Tribune, the San Jose Mercury News*, and the *New York Times* among others.

AOL has a special kids' section called *Kids Only* that has super graphics, offers *Disney Adventures Magazine*, online games, a competitive trivia test, and a "Kids Only" bulletin board for kids to talk about their favorite subjects. *Kids Only* caters more to middle-grade and teenage users rather than younger kids. But in general they get high marks for both their easy-to-use graphic interface and content.

COMPUSERVE

Contact: 800-848-8199

Users: 1.8 million

Cost: There are two price plans currently available: CompuServe's standard pricing plan is $9.95/month, and includes access to their basic services, including hundreds of forums and discussion groups, and file libraries. You can also access *U.S. News & World Report, CNN,* and the *Detroit Free Press.* For surfing the Internet, you get 3 free hours each month, with $2.50 for additional hours. Each hour costs $4.80. Also, you get a $9 monthly Mail Allowance. This allows you to send approximately 90 three-page full-text messages per month.

The other plan, designed for heavy Internet users, offers 20 hours of access for $15 a month, in addition to the basic $9.95 monthly membership charge. Additional hours will cost $1.95 per hour. E-mail is billed at the hourly connect charges.

Internet services that CompuServe currently offers include: World Wide Web, File Transfer Protocol (FTP), Telnet, and Usenet Newsgroups. No IRC service. To find CompuServe's area for kids, just type in the key words, *Go: STUDENTS*

DELPHI

Contact: 800-695-4005
Users: 500,0000
Cost: Delphi currently offers two pricing plans: A "10–4 Plan," which costs $10 for 4 hours a month, with each additional hour at $4. A "20–20 Plan," which provides 20 hours per month with additional hours at $1.80. There is a $19 enrollment fee except during trial periods, when it's $9.

You get 10 hours of free time to try it out. Both plans have a $3 per month charge for Internet access. There are additional surcharges for access through Tymnet or SprintNet phone lines during business hours (6 A.M. to 6 P.M.) of $9 per hour. Delphi offers complete Internet access.

Their service also includes the *Orange County Register,* the *St. Louis Post-Dispatch,* and stories from *Reuters, Variety, Billboard,* and the *Hollywood Reporter.* If you're after more complete Internet access and can do without the bells and whistles, Delphi is a good choice.

PRODIGY

Contact: 800-776-3499

Users: 1.7 million

Cost: Prodigy currently has 3 plans: The basic plan, at $9.95 per month minimum for up to five hours, $2.95 each additional hour, includes basic features of e-mail and forums. The Value Plan, at $14.95 for unlimited use of basic features, as well as five hours per month of Plus Features, including chat, airline reservations, and Internet access. Additional hours at $2.95.

The 30–30 Plan with 30 free hours of Plus and Core services at $29.95 a month.

Prodigy also offers *Newsweek,* the *Los Angeles Times,* and *Sports Illustrated for Kids.* Prodigy offers one of the best-looking World Wide Web browsers, in addition to FTP, Telnet, newsgroups, and e-mail. They also have a kids' area online which includes the *Sesame Street* cast of characters such as Bert, Ernie, the Count, and Big Bird. Key in *Jump: KIDS* to get there. An online version of the popular *Where in the World Is Carmen Sandiego?* is great for learning geography. One glitch in all the graphics is that navigating through the basic Prodigy services can sometimes be slow.

EWORLD

Contact: 800-775-4556

Users: 100,000

Cost: Currently $8.95 a month.

At the moment eWorld, which only supports Apple computers, has a graphic interface that looks like AOL. They should be on the Internet by the time this book appears. A lot of kids use eWorld, and if you are a Macintosh™ user, you should definitely give them a call.

In addition to these services, both IBM™ and Microsoft™ are currently establishing their own Internet services.

INTERNET-ONLY PROVIDERS

With the rapid spread of interest in the Internet, more and more companies have begun to provide nationwide Internet access. That means you can subscribe to a service in your hometown and access the Internet through a local phone number. Then when you visit your aunt in Connecticut (if you have an aunt in Connecticut!), that service will provide you with a local Connecticut telephone number.

The Internet-only providers don't offer the forums, files, and other goodies of the commercial services, but for folks who just want to surf the Internet, they tend to be less expensive.

PSI PIPELINE USA

Contact: 800-453-PIPE

Cost: Currently $19.95 a month for unlimited online time. Pipeline used to be just a New York provider, but they were bought out by PSI and are now national. They offer all the usual services, except IRC, but their Web browser isn't up to the quality of Netscape™ or the browsers on the major online services. Still this is an excellent start-up package to consider for surfing the Net.

PSI INTERRAMP

Contact: 800-82-PSI-82

Cost: Interramp currently costs $99 for setup, and they provide the software. That price includes the first month of service. After the first month, their rate is $9/month for 9 hours, or $29 for 29 hours, $1.50 per hour over that. Interramp is owned by

PSI, which also owns Pipeline, and the difference between the services is that with Interramp you can use any software package.

NETCOM NETCRUISER

Contact: 800-353-6600

Cost: Netcruiser currently costs $25 for setup and their rate is $19.95 a month for 40 peak hours. Time online between midnight and 9:00 A.M. and weekends is free. Netcruiser™ is Netcom's software package and includes all the Internet tools, including IRC. Like Interramp, you can also use your own software packages if you prefer. Netcruiser is very similar to Pipeline in presenting a totally integrated screen to make it easy to navigate the Net. Currently they support only Windows™, but they expect to have a Macintosh™ package by the end of 1995.

LOCAL PROVIDERS

Finally, local providers are the least expensive but sometimes the most complicated way of getting on the Internet.

Local providers only offer service in one town or city, with only one or two local phone numbers. Most will not provide their own software, although they will give you shareware versions of popular Internet programs for World Wide Web, e-mail, and Usenet browsing. Most will also spend time on the phone helping you get your programs up and running and often have printed help instructions that they will send you to.

The average cost for a local provider is between $20 and $35 a month for unlimited access.

For a local Internet service provider in your area, look in your telephone book under *Computers*. You can also call a computer store. Many cities have local computer magazines or technology sections in the newspaper where local providers often advertise.

If you plan to be online more than 20 or 30 hours per month, then an Internet-only service provider may be your most economical choice.

The following chart compares the Internet charges based on the hours used per month.

	Basic Services	Internet Hours	Additional Hours
AOL	$9.95	5	$2.95 hr
COMPU	$25.95	20	$1.95 hr (Net) $4.80 hr (basic)
PRODIGY	$9.95	30	$2.95
NETCOM	$19.95	40	$2.00 hr
PIPELINE	$19.95	unlimited	
INTERRAMP	$29.00	29	$2.00 hr

If you expect to be online fewer than 20 hours a month, then a commercial online service costs about the same as an Internet gateway provider. But if you plan to be online for an hour a day or more, then the cost of using a commercial online service begins to rise.

Most services, both national and local, will offer a free trial period, from a few hours to a few days, in which to try them out. Be aware that almost all the services require billing by credit card, so you'll have to have your parents' cooperation. After the trial period, don't forget to keep an eye on the clock!

If you decide to use an Internet service provider instead of a commercial service like CompuServe or Prodigy, here are some questions to ask:

1. Do you bill by credit card or send a statement?

2. What are the rates per month? What happens if I use more than my allotted time?

3. How can I find out at any given time how many hours I have used?

4. How many subscribers do you have?

5. How many incoming calls can you handle?

6. Do you have a local telephone number? (This is important if your provider is national and not local.)

7. Can I call you to get help if I need it? When can I call?

8. Can I try the service for free to see if I like it?

9. What Internet services do you offer? (E-mail, Gopher, FTP, Usenet, Telnet, World Wide Web, and IRC are the ones to ask for.)

10. Do you provide Macintosh™ and/or Windows™ software for all the services you offer?

11. What modems do you provide software for? What is the suggested minimum baud rate? Maximum baud rate?

12. What is the amount of memory required for my computer to run effectively using your service?

NOTE: When you finally do get online and receive all your software, be sure to record your Internet gateway information in the charts provided in the next chapter of this book.

Chapter 9

Recording Your Internet Gateway Information:

Plus 4 Charts to Personalize

Here are four charts for you to record your Internet gateway information. As soon as you get this information from your online provider or service, copy it down here for safekeeping. If you change your service or add a new service, we have provided a few extra charts.

INTERNET GATEWAY PROVIDER RECORD

Name of provider: _____

Tech support phone number: _____

Log on phone number(s):_____

_____

Domain name of provider: _____

Interface name: _____

IP (Internet Protocol) address:_____

Log on user name: _____

Log on password: _____

Mail server name: _____

Mail password:_____

News server:_____

Domain servers: _____

_____

Gateway address: _____

Modem (type and speed):_____

Port (com port of your modem):_____

Additional notes:_____

_____

_____

_____

_____

_____

_____

INTERNET GATEWAY PROVIDER RECORD

Name of provider: _____

Tech support phone number: _____

Log on phone number(s): _____

_____

Domain name of provider: _____

Interface name: _____

IP (Internet Protocol) address: _____

Log on user name: _____

Log on password: _____

Mail server name: _____

Mail password: _____

News server: _____

Domain servers: _____

_____

Gateway address: _____

Modem (type and speed): _____

Port (com port of your modem): _____

Additional notes: _____

_____

_____

_____

_____

_____

_____

INTERNET GATEWAY PROVIDER RECORD

Name of provider: _____

Tech support phone number: _____

Log on phone number(s): _____

_____

Domain name of provider: _____

Interface name: _____

IP (Internet Protocol) address: _____

Log on user name: _____

Log on password: _____

Mail server name: _____

Mail password: _____

News server: _____

Domain servers: _____

_____

Gateway address: _____

Modem (type and speed): _____

Port (com port of your modem): _____

Additional notes: _____

_____

_____

_____

_____

_____

_____

INTERNET GATEWAY PROVIDER RECORD

Name of provider: _____

Tech support phone number: _____

Log on phone number(s): _____

_____

Domain name of provider: _____

Interface name: _____

IP (Internet Protocol) address: _____

Log on user name: _____

Log on password: _____

Mail server name: _____

Mail password: _____

News server: _____

Domain servers: _____

_____

Gateway address: _____

Modem (type and speed): _____

Port (com port of your modem): _____

Additional notes: _____

_____

_____

_____

_____

_____

_____

Chapter 10

Parents' Guide:

Where Are Your Kids Tonight on the Internet?

CyberSarge is a fictitious cartoon guy who has been taking your kids on a tour of the Internet. Your kids already know and respect him a great deal for he has taught them a lot. If they've followed the book through to this point, they've even been promoted from Cadets to full-fledged Internauts. Now it's time for you to meet him. And he has some notes specifically for parents and teachers. That's what this section is all about. Kids are welcome to read it, too.

Since most Internet providers require that an adult sign up for the Internet service by pledging to pay monthly fees and other charges billed directly through a credit card, parents must be involved to a certain extent in their children's travels in cyberspace. As well, hooking up to the Internet involves using a modem; unless you have a dedicated telephone line just for computer use, your phone line will be tied up whenever your kids are on the Internet. Having read through this book, your kids know that. And we have already covered many of these issues with your children so we won't repeat them here. [See the sections in Chapter 2: Preparing for Liftoff, starting on page 41, and Chapter 5: The Top Ten Rules for Surfing the Net, starting on page 101, which suggests ways for children and parents to discuss Internet access.]

However, CyberSarge believes that parents have a lot bigger stake than just money and telephone time in their kids' involvement on the Internet. Assuming you parents and teachers are not already surfing the Net yourselves, your children will be introducing you to a new world with which many adults are only vaguely familiar. CyberSarge thinks that it would be a great idea for you to browse through this book as well. But if you don't have the time or the inclination, or even if you have already read this along with your kids, there are some issues that you should be aware of.

So let's go online with CyberSarge and hear what he has to say.

| File | Edit | View |

ISSUES FOR GROWN-UPS

While cyberspace may seem strange and mysterious, sometimes making you feel like Dorothy in the Land of Oz or the inimitable Alice in that odd place called Wonderland, the Internet is just like the rest of our world.

Like your cities and neighborhoods, the Internet is OK most of the time. But there are still a few hidden dangers to watch out for—just as you watch out for potholes in the road when you're driving.

Watching your kids venture into the Internet is a bit like sending them off to school for the first time. Just as you teach your children to look both ways when crossing the street and not to accept rides from strangers, there are rules your children need to know when they are navigating the Net.

Your kids are entering a new and exciting place. And as parents and educators, you need to know what to look out for so you can advise them.

First of all, think of the Internet as a giant shopping mall. There are places in the mall that are OK for your kids to go into and some places you've told them to stay away from. There are movies they can see, and movies they can't. There are rules, and as parents and teachers you've set up those rules and you expect your kids to follow them. When they don't, they're punished or "grounded." It's the same way on the Internet. And being online is a privilege that you have allowed your children to participate in.

If your kids' connection to the Internet is through a commercial service like CompuServe or America Online, you should know that the administrators of these services take reasonable precautions to keep truly objectionable or offensive messages off their systems. But once in cyberspace on the Internet, whether through a commercial service or an Internet gateway provider, there are as yet no real barricades to keep children out of places they shouldn't be.

But that shouldn't frighten you. The real world is the same way. And the same rules that you would apply to dealing with kids in the real world apply to the Internet.

Let's talk for a minute about the dangers on the Internet, and the things you and your children can do to avoid them.

The first thing to remember is that the Internet is normally accessed through a phone line. When you answer the phone at home, if something or someone bothers you, you can just hang up. You can do the same thing on the Internet: hang up, or go somewhere else.

The Internet is a "network of networks," meaning that there are millions of users all connected to one another through phone lines and computers in that vast unseeable place called cyberspace. One of the benefits of the Internet is that it is a forum where information is shared widely and freely and where educational material is literally at your fingertips. However, that freedom can also be a source of potential mischief.

There is no one in charge who is overseeing all the messages and files that are posted every second of the day. Some newsgroups are moderated. That means there is a person in charge to keep the discussion on track and rein in "flamers," or people who pick fights or post inappropriate or obscene messages. But many more groups are not moderated. You can usually tell from the name of a list or newsgroup if it's something you want your kids to be reading. Fortunately, there are special forums set up for kids only that are monitored all the time. [To find out if your provider has a kids' forum, refer to Chapter 8: Finding Your Cybership, starting on page 151. If you are still not sure, simply telephone or e-mail the online service you have chosen and they will provide that information.]

In addition, while the vast majority of folks on the Internet are OK, a very few may not be. There are people whose main objective in life seems to be to go online and start fights. There are others who want to demean or belittle others, perhaps so they can feel superior. And a very few seek to exploit or even to harm others.

That's a bit frightening, and it's easy to overreact—especially when you're facing a new technology that your children may seem to understand better than you do. The outside world has gotten more dangerous since you were a child—but that's no reason to stay indoors.

What is needed on the street is **street smarts.** What you and your children need on the Internet is **cybersmarts**.

One risk you must consider: Your child may be exposed to inappropriate material of a sexual or violent nature.

A second risk is that your child might provide personal information while online that could risk his or her safety, or the safety of other family members.

A third risk is that your children might receive e-mail messages that are harassing, demeaning, or sexual.

To help restrict your child's access to areas that contain inappropriate material, many of the commercial online services and some of the Internet gateway service providers have systems in place for parents to block out parts of the service they feel are inappropriate for their children. This is just like locking out certain phone numbers or cable TV channels.

If you are concerned, you should contact the service you're using or thinking of using, by telephone or e-mail to find out how you can add these restrictions to any accounts that your children can access.

The U.S. government is also in the process of evaluating obscenity and pornography use on the Internet. Cybercops, or secret service personnel who travel cyberspace, do prosecute some offenders. However, the Internet is a rather anarchical entity, changing every day. There is no way to keep up with all of the new information posted or to chase down every online flamer.

Therefore, the best way to assure that your children are having positive online experiences is to stay in touch with what they are doing. You can do this by spending time with your children while they're online. Have them show you what they do, and ask them to teach you how to access the services they use.

Keep in mind that while children need a certain amount of privacy, they also need parental involvement and supervision in their daily lives.

The same general parenting skills that apply to the "real world" also apply while your kids are in cyberspace. If you have cause for concern about your children's online activities, discuss it with them.

Seek out the advice and counsel of other computer users in your area. Talk with your child's teacher or other parents and become familiar with the literature on the Internet. Open communication with your children is important. Also, the use of the same computer resources your children use and getting online yourself will help you obtain the full benefits of these resources. Who knows, you might even have as much fun and learn as much as they are! And being online yourself may alert you to potential problems that may occur there.

By taking responsibility for your children's online computer use, you can greatly minimize the potential risks involved in being online.

You should get to know the Internet services your child uses. If you don't know how to log on, get your child to show you. Become familiar with their online friends just as you would get to know all of their other friends.

Make it a firm rule that your children never give out identifying information—home address, school name, last names, parents' names or work places, or telephone numbers—in a public message such as a chat or bulletin board. In fact, they should never reveal this personal information online, for there are some computer users, called **hackers**, who can access even "private" communications between other users. [See Chapter 5: The Top Ten Rules for Surfing the Net, starting on page 101.]

Making new friends is great, and it's OK to make new friends online. But you should never allow your child to arrange a face-to-face meeting with another computer user. No matter how harmless a face-to-face meeting might seem, it is absolutely **not** a good idea.

If you or your child receives a message that is harassing, of a sexual nature, or threatening, forward a copy of the message to your online service provider and ask for their assistance.

The bottom line is that it's up to you, as parents and teachers, to set reasonable rules and guidelines for computer use by your children. Discuss these rules and post them near the computer as a reminder. Remember to monitor their compliance with these rules, especially when it comes to the amount of time your children spend on the computer.

You might consider keeping the computer in a family room rather than your child's bedroom. That way you can all share the experience of going online.

We've provided a contract for you and your children to sign on the following page. Copy it and put it somewhere near the computer so that your children will be reminded that they have promised to follow the house rules of surfing the Internet.

Make the Internet a family activity and you'll all enjoy the experience that much more.

Have fun surfing the Net,

CyberSarge

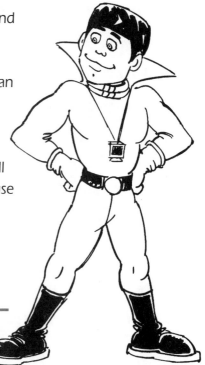

OFFICIAL INTERNET CONTRACT

I, _____, Cyberspace Internaut, do solemnly swear

that I will surf the Net for no more than _____ hours a day or a total of

_____ hours per week.

I promise to keep my parents or teacher informed of all my activity
on the Internet.

I promise to obey the Top Ten Rules for Surfing the Net, including:

1. Never giving out personal information.

2. Avoiding unpleasant situations.

3. Always being myself.

4. Always sticking to my budget.

5. Always expressing myself but staying cool.

6. Always treating newbies as I would want to be treated.

7. Always using my common sense.

8. Always treating people online with respect.

9. Always sharing ideas, files, and helpful opinions.

10. Being an active and useful member of Cyberspace.

I also agree to the following:

_____

_____

_____

_____

_____   _____
First Official Cyberspace Internaut   **Date**

_____   _____
Grown-up   **Date**

Chapter 11

Glossary:

More Technical (But Fun!) Terms You Might Come Across

Here's CyberSarge's dictionary of more cyberspeak terms so that you can talk the talk when you're on the Net. If you want to see where we talk about a word in context, you'll find other entries for it in the Index of Terms, starting on page 199.

Acronyms are shortcuts in which a phrase is represented by its initials. For instance, FTP stands for File Transfer Protocol.

Address. An Internet address is just like your home or apartment address, only it is in cyberspace. Once you have an Internet address, you have a place all your own on the Internet. All the Internet addresses given in this book are in ***bold italics*** to make sure the punctuation in them is not confused with regular punctuation. You do not need to use **bold** nor ***italics*** when typing in any Internet addresses.

Archie is a computer software program that lets you type in a key word to search for things. You can use Archie to search thousands of FTP databases all over the world for the file or files that contain the information you are looking for.

Articles. Letters that are posted in newsgroups are often referred to as articles rather than letters. This is because in mailing lists you are usually answering one person—even though everyone on the mailing list can read your letter. But in newsgroups you are often writing comments to the whole group, much like a reporter writes an article for everyone who subscribes to a magazine.

ASCII is an acronym that stands for American Standard Code for Information Interchange. It was created so that there would be a standard language to transfer files between different types of programs and computers. In practice, ASCII text is plain, unformatted text that can be read by any computer's word processor. It's pronounced "ask-key."

Artificial reality is similar to virtual reality, but more interactive, with the participant being an active part of, not just experiencing, the artificial environment, often being allowed to change that environment.

Baud is the speed at which modems transfer data. One baud is roughly equal to one bit per second. It takes eight bits to make up one letter or character on your keyboard.

Baud rate is a measurement of data transmission speed. Baud rate is sometimes measured in *bits per second.* Your modem may have a baud rate of 14.4 Kbs (Kilobytes). This translates to 14,400 bits per second (the capital K stands for thousand).

BBS. See **Bulletin Board Systems.**

Binary refers to a number system that uses only a 1 or 0. It is this system which is used by computers to transfer files.

Bit is the smallest unit of information that can be sent between computers. Computers store all information in a binary system that consists of bits. A bit is 0 or 1, off or on. Eight bits make a byte.

Bookmarks are markers that allow you to mark a Gopher menu or a World Wide Web page that you like so you can return to that menu or page whenever you want. All of your bookmarks are kept in a booklist that acts just like your own personal menu.

Boot up. You do this when you start up your computer by turning on the power.

Bounce is what your e-mail does when it cannot get to where you tried to send it. It either bounces back to you, or goes off into deep cyberspace, never to be found again.

Bulletin Board Systems (BBS) are networks that your computer can dial into through your modem. You communicate with other people by exchanging messages and files. You can also take pictures and information that the bulletin board operator puts up for public use and download these to your own computer for later viewing.

Byte is the number of bits needed to represent a letter (a, b, c) or number (1, 2, 3). A byte is eight bits.

CERT is the Computer Emergency Response Team. It is a security force for the Internet that maintains a clearinghouse for information about network security, including attempted—or successful—break-ins to private computer systems.

Chat. An online chat is a lot like talking to someone on the phone in real time, only you type out your words on your computer rather than speak out loud.

Click on means you point at something on the screen with your mouse pointer—a picture, icon, or hypertext link—and press down on the mouse button.

Command line is where you tell the computer (usually on a UNIX™ system) what you want it to do, by entering commands.

Commercial service access. The most popular commercial online services—America Online, CompuServe, Delphi, eWorld and Prodigy—all have gateways into the Internet. Any of these services can be a good way to start surfing the Net since they have simple icons that make it easy to get help when you're online. You also have access to their other services as well, including e-mail, for which they will provide the software.

Computer language. A computer language is a system that allows different types of computers to speak to each other. Basically, computers translate English (or Spanish, or Arabic, or any other human language) into numbers because every computer can understand numbers.

Cursor. The cursor is usually a blinking box or line on your computer screen. It indicates where the next character you type in will be inserted.

Cybercops. (See **Datacops**.)

Cyberian is an online librarian who makes a living doing information research and retrieval. Because of their experience, cyberians are considered to be really hot data surfers.

Cyberpunk is a subcategory of science fiction, first launched in 1982 by William Gibson's novel, *Neuromancer*.

Cyberspace is that place where people and computers meet. Cyberspace is where you go when you go online. It's the universe that exists inside computer networks. You can't see it, but it's there—and you can visit it.

Data is information that has been formatted so that it can be understood by a computer. Data can include text, numbers, program codes, graphic art, sound, or even video clips.

Databases. Think of these as electronic file cabinets containing data—or information—that is all related to a single topic or can be put into a specific catagory. A hospital's database might contain information on all the patients in that hospital, or a school's database would contain information on all the students attending that school.

Datacops can be any agency that protects data. Most often it refers to U.S. Secret Service agents who are also known as Cybercops.

Deck cowboys are futuristic—some say fantasy—versions of a computer hacker.

Delurking is when you come out of your shell and join the party.

Digital. Computers "talk" to other computers digitally. That is they store and process information as a series of numbers. Anything—including words, pictures, and sounds—can be "digitized" into the computer, then "undigitized" with a software program—like a word processor—so you can read the words, hear the sounds, or see the pictures.

Directory. The hard disk on your computer is divided into directories. Each directory can contain many different files. If you think of your computer's hard disk like a file cabinet, then directories are drawers in that cabinet.

Disk drive. This is the part of the computer that transfers the information on your floppy disk into the computer's memory, or transfers what is in the computer's memory onto your hard disk. Think of this like a tape recorder that can play what is on the tape or can record music or words and put them on the tape. Disk drives come in two formats: a hard drive and a floppy drive.

Documents are more than just text. Think of computer documents as magazine articles or newspaper stories. There is the story, but there may also be pictures or maps or video clips to help you better understand the text.

Domain name is the name given to a host computer on the Internet. The host computer is connected directly to the Internet.

Dot is what you say instead of "period," when you are talking about Internet addresses. For example, "My Internet address is Zack at mynet dot com."

Down is what happens when a computer site runs into technical trouble and you can no longer gain access to it.

Download. When you download you are recieving information to your computer from another computer, usually through a modem.

Dweeb is a put-down description of someone who is really out of it.

E-mail is "electronic mail," which just means that it is sent by the computer rather than through your local post office. It doesn't even need a postage stamp, and it gets there a lot faster than "snail mail."

Escape character is a keyboard command that allows you to exit a computer system in case that system crashes or gets into a loop.

FAQs are Frequently Asked Questions. They're the best place to start when you're curious about a subject. The names for these files usually end with *.faq*.

Feeb is a real incompetent at something, as in "I'm a real feeb when it comes to math."

Fiber optic cable is a new type of high-speed cable that is much smaller than the old, copper-wire cables used for telephone lines. These new cables can carry much more information at much faster speeds. Most long-distance phone traffic is already carried in digital form, through high-volume fiber optic cables.

File. Think of a file like a folder on your computer that can hold documents, programs, pictures, or other types of computer data.

File Transfer Protocol, or FTP, is a part of a software program that allows you to get files—which might be documents or software programs—from other computers, or to send files to other computers.

Filters are used by software programs to send information to a particular place so you don't have to do it by hand. Filters work just like coin sorters work: You feed any coin into the opening and the machine directs the nickels to one slot, dimes to another, pennies to another, and so on.

Flaming is stomping on someone in cyberspace for saying something you consider wrong or just plain stupid, without being reasonable. It's kind of like slamming the door when you're mad.

Floppy disk. This is a flexible plastic covered disk (usually 3.5 or 5.25 inches in size) that is inserted into a computer's floppy disk drive and used to transfer or store information. These are also called *diskettes*.

Floppy drive. This is a disk drive that reads and writes from floppy disks. You stick a floppy disk into this drive.

Forum. In online services a forum is a special place for discussing a certain subject.

Freenet is a bulletin board system that is connected to the Internet and is free of charge. Usually these are sponsored by community groups to give people free access to computing and information.

Freeware is software that you use and give to your friends without paying for it—and it's OK to do so.

FTP. (See **File Transfer Protocol**)

Gateway. A gateway is a computer system that acts as a translator between different types of computers to allow them to interact in cyberspace.

Gateway servers are computers that allow you access to the Internet.

Geeks are people who are really excited by computers and are proud of it.

Geek speak refers to words that are usually only used in reference to computers and being on the Internet.

GIF stands for Graphic Interchange Format, a format developed by CompuServe for use in storing photo-quality graphic images. It's now commonly used everywhere online.

Gigabyte. A gigabyte is a billion bytes. A gigabyte looks like 1,000,000,000 bytes.

Gopher™ is a very popular Internet software program that lets you look through all kinds of online libraries for information.

Gopher server. This is a computer on the Internet that is set up to service the information requests issued by the Gopher™ program. Gopher programs—also called *search engines*—help you find information you are looking for in cyberspace.

Gopherspace is simply another word for cyberspace. Specifically, Gopherspace is anywhere on the Internet that a Gopher program can go to.

Graphical browser is a program that allows you to search for documents and sites with pictures in them.

Graphical sites are places in cyberspace that have pictures or links to other places, pictures, and movies. The World Wide Web is one of the best places to find graphical sites.

Graphics are images and pictures.

Hacker. This is slang for someone who may have a degree in computer science, but who has gained most of his or her computer expertise through trial and error, learning to navigate in cyberspace in places not usually taught about in computer classes.

Handshake is what two modems trying to connect first do to agree on how to transfer data.

Hang is what happens when a modem fails to hang up or a computer fails to respond to mouse clicks or keystrokes.

Hard copy refers to printing out a paper copy of a computer document on a printer.

Hard disk. This is a magnetic disk that stores information and is permanently installed in your computer. Hard disks can hold much more information than floppy disks. They are also sometimes called *fixed disks*.

Hard drive. This is a disk drive that reads and writes from hard disks.

Headers are phrases at the start of a message that tell you what the message is about. They are like headlines in a newspaper that tell you what a particular news story is about.

Highlighted means that a word or phrase is marked so that it stands out. The word might be in *italics* or **bolded**. On the Web highlighted words and phrases are hyperlinks that can take you to other locations.

Host. This is a computer that is connected directly to the Internet. Like a restaurant host who invites you into a restaurant and often seats you, a host computer acts as your gateway onto the Net.

Hotlist is the same as a bookmark.

Hyperlink. This is the connection address used in hypertext documents to jump from one element to another.

Hypermedia is hypertext with pictures and sounds, as well as words. Your computer screen might display images with sound or animated cartoons instead of text—all with pointers leading you to other locations where you'll find even *more* images, sounds, and text!

Hypertext is specially formatted text used in World Wide Web documents. When you click on or choose this text, you will jump to the Web page that the hypertext is linked to. That new page will very likely have a hyperlink to take you back to your starting point. You can travel all over the Web this way, always able to jump back to where you began.

HyperText Markup Language (HTML) is the programming language used to create hyperlinks on the Web.

Icon. This is a small image on the computer screen that executes a program or a function within a larger program when you point and click on it with your mouse pointer. Icons are pictures that represent the program or type of function in the software.

Ident is cybertalk shorthand for *identity*.

Identity hacking is the use of pseudo-anonymity or false accounts to pretend to be another person on the Internet. It's not a nice thing to do.

Index file. Most FTP directories have this special file. The Index file is a list of what information is contained in each file on that particular computer. Think of an Index file like the index at the back of a book, telling you where in the book to go to find out about a particular subject or to find out the definition of a particular word.

Install. This means setting up a software program so that it runs on your computer.

Installation program. This is a program that often comes with software to set it up on your computer. Sometimes it is called a *setup program*.

Interactive. This describes the two-way dialogue between computer programs and you. In other words, when you do something on your computer, the computer responds and then returns control back to you. Interactive computer games are games in which you can affect the outcome or final result.

Internauts. These are astronauts who are exploring the new frontiers of *cyber*space rather than outer space.

Internet. In the beginning there was the ARPANET, a wide area experimental network that linked universities and government research labs together. Over time other groups formed their own networks. The collection of all of these different networks linked together became what we call the Internet.

Key pals are pen pals that you communicate with to through the computer. Since you use a keyboard to type your e-mail letters, pen pals in cyberspace are called *key pals*.

Key words. Most documents contain specific or "key" words that tell you a bit about what the document is about. For example, the words *baseball, pitcher,* and *World Series* would tell you that the document is about World Series baseball pitchers.

Leased line access. This is really the same as a SLIP/PPP account except that you are using a high speed, direct line instead of a regular phone line to go online. It's much faster, but also much more expensive. But the speed of traveling the Internet—which can be five to ten times faster with leased-line access than with a regular modem—may make this worthwhile if you have a lot of surfing to do.

Links are addresses that are inserted into hypertext documents that let you jump to another document. (See **Hypertext**.)

Listserver. A listserver is a program that automatically sends and receives e-mail to and from a particular group of subscribers.

Listserver mailing list is like a subscription to an online magazine. When you join up, you can get information on whatever subject you've chosen; and you get updates regularly. These are designed for many people to use who share similar interests and want to exchange messages with each other. Listserver mailing lists are maintained by an automated postmaster, or *Listserv* program. Usually you do not participate in writing the information that is sent out to all the subscribers.

Log off is what you do when you leave the remote computer. You usually log off by typing or clicking *bye, exit, goodbye,* or *quit.*

Log on means to connect to a remote computer system. (*Log in* means the same thing as *log on*.)

Loop. A computer loop is what happens when you get in a series of repeating commands, so you end up running around in endless circles. This usually causes your computer to crash or freeze, meaning that you have to restart your computer to get it running again.

Lurking means hanging around in the background and watching without getting involved. Most of us are lurkers when we first enter a new neighborhood on the Internet.

Mainframes. These are large computers— sometimes taking up a whole room!— that are usually found in big companies and colleges, and that are used by many people. Mainframes are expensive and often need special air-conditioned rooms. While many mainframes are still being used, they are rapidly being replaced by smaller computers, even by personal computers like yours.

Modem stands for "modulator-demodulator." It's a device that allows your computer to link up with other computers over telephone lines.

Mouse. A mouse is a hand-held device used to move the cursor (the blinking line or arrow that tells you where you are) around the computer screen. A mouse has one, two, or three buttons that are used to execute commands. Other devices have balls on them to move the cursor, and some newer ones have pads that trace the movement of your finger to move the cursor.

MUD is a Multiple User Dimensional game. MUDs are role-playing games that exist on the Internet for entertainment purposes. MUDs are mostly text-based virtual worlds which many players (participants) may explore, change, or add on to the game at the same time. In most cases, the MUD is actually a game with scores, player attributes, levels, etc., but some MUDs have more social goals in mind. MUDs are usually based on different science-fiction genres such as fantasy, space, or even cyberpunk.

Net is short for *Internet*.

Netiquette is simply the proper way to behave when you're surfing the Internet, such as respecting the rights and opinions of others, and treating others the way you want to be treated.

Network is a group of computers joined by data-carrying links. A network may be as small as two or three personal computers tied together by telephone lines in the same building, or it may be a vast complex of computers spread across the world, whose data links include telephone lines, satellite relays, fiber optic cables, or radio links.

Newbie is what we all are sometime or another when we're just starting to learn our way around in cyberspace.

Newsreader software programs usually come with your Internet service package and allow you to read the news available in newsgroups.

Newsgroups are online gatherings in which you can discuss almost any subject you can imagine—from how to house-train your pet to what the latest UFO rumor is. There are currently over 10,000 active newsgroups. (See **Usenet**.)

NNTP. NNTP stands for Network News Transfer Protocol. These are local servers which distribute Usenet newsgroups throughout the globe.

NSF is the National Science Foundation. They fund the NSFNet, a high-speed network that once formed the backbone of the Internet in the United States.

Offline means you're not connected to another computer system.

Ohnosecond is that terrible moment in time when you realize you've just made a BIG mistake—like erasing all the files in the *wrong* subdirectory.

Online means you are connected to another computer system.

Password. A password is a secret name that you and only you know. After you enter your user name, you are asked to enter your secret name, that way no one can get onto a network and pretend to be you.

Paste. This means clipping sections from one file and putting them into another.

Peripheral is an extra device, like a modem or printer, that you can attach to your computer.

Ping™ is a program that can trace the route a message takes through the Internet from your computer to another computer.

POP stands for Post Office Protocol. POP is a system that allows Internet mail servers to act just like a real post office. POPs look at the mail that arrives and route it toward its final destination.

Port is the plug in the back of your computer where you can attach a modem, a printer, a mouse, or other peripherals. Port also refers to a number that identifies a particular Internet service (for instance, Port 6667 usually means an IRC server).

PPP stands for Point-to-Point Protocol, a way that computers talk to one another over the Internet. (See **SLIP**).

Prompt is when the computer asks you to do something and waits for you to respond. For example, if you see *login:* or *log on:* the computer is waiting for you to type in your user name.

Public domain means that no one owns something, such as some software programs available on the Net. When something is public domain, it is free to anyone who wants to get and use it.

Readme files are files, often found on FTP sites, that explain what is in an FTP directory or that provide other useful information. You also get readme files with computer software, often explaining things you need to know that are not in the printed instruction manual.

Protocol is a set of rules for computers to talk to one another over a network.

Real time refers to actual time. In terms of the Internet, it means that you can get an instant response to whatever you do. Think of how you speak on the phone versus how you send a paper letter through snail mail; when you're on the phone you get instant responses—in real time—from the person on the other end to whatever you say. When you send a letter through snail mail, you have to wait for it to get picked up by the postal carrier, taken to the post office, and delivered before you can get a response.

Remote computer is a computer connected to your computer via telephone lines (or via other network connections).

Search capabilities. This just means that there exists an index that can be searched. Think of it as the card files in your local library. You can search through them to see if there are books in the library on the subject you are interested in.

Search engines are programs that are designed to go out onto the Internet and search for the information you requested. Think of them as librarians who give you a list of possible books to read to find out what you want to know, then go help you find the books.

Search words. Documents contain specific words in them that tell you a bit about the subject they are discussing. For example, if you use the search words *baseball, pitcher*, and *World Series,* you would find documents that have those words in them. Chances are that a document that has all three of those words would be about World Series baseball pitchers.

Server is a computer that provides a particular service over the Internet, such as e-mail, chat, or FTP. Think of a server like a receptionist in an office; the receptionist knows where to direct all the calls that come in.

Service provider is an organization, such as America Online, or Interramp, that provides access to the Internet.

Set up. This means installing a software program on your computer.

Shareware is like freeware and it doesn't cost you anything to get and try it out. But if you like it and want to use it, then the author of the program asks for a small licensing fee.

Shell account access. An Internet gateway, this is the simplest way to go online. It's almost like logging on to a local computer bulletin board system. You can send e-mail messages and download files. Most shell accounts have very little or no graphics, and often they require you to learn UNIX™ commands to operate them. Shell accounts usually aren't very pretty, but they are cheap.

Site. This refers to the physical location of a computer. The word is sometimes used to refer to where a computer is located in cyberspace as well. For instance, when you go to MyNet's site, you are going (either through the Internet, or physically by walking or taking a bus) to the place where the MyNet computer exists.

SLIP is Serial Line Interface Protocol, another way that computers talk to one another over the Internet (See **PPP**).

SLIP/PPP dial up access. SLIP (Serial Line Interface Protocol) and PPP (Point-to-Point Protocol) are a step up from a shell account. Here you are connected directly to the Internet through a service provider which has a computer gateway into the Internet and will let you use it for a price. There are national providers that give you the basic Internet services through their own software. There are also national and local providers that give you a software package or let you use your own.

Smiley. When you're face-to-face, you can smile, frown, or make a multitude of facial expressions to enhance your words. You can also sound happy, sad, angry, or just plain bored. In e-mail your words have to carry your thoughts by themselves, so folks invented smileys to punctuate their phrases. They are also called "emoticons" (short for "emotion" and "icon"). There are two types of basic smileys: those with words and those with pictures.

SMTP stands for Simple Mail Transfer Protocol. SMTP is the language Internet mail servers (or postmasters) use to talk to one another and to exchange e-mail letters.

Snail mail is the paper mail that comes through a slot in your front door or is deposited in a box mounted outside your house or apartment.

Software program. These are the instructions that tell the computer how to do what you want it to do.

SPAM stands for Sending Particularly Annoying Messages. Spamming is sending an article *everywhere* on the Internet. Instead of sending an article to specific groups that might be interested in it, you send it to anyone and everyone. This is not nice. Don't clutter up the Internet with junk mail.

Supercomputer. This is a mainframe-sized computer that operates much faster than a normal desktop or laptop computer, and is used for special science and military projects.

Surfing. Traveling through cyberspace via your computer is often called *surfing*.

Sysadmin is the system administrator, who is the person who runs a computer site. Often used to mean the same thing as *sysop*, or system operator.

Sysop is the SYStem OPerator, someone who runs a computer system or bulletin board.

TCP/IP is an acronym for Transmission Control Protocol/Internet Protocol. These are a bunch of communication rules developed by the University of California for the Department of Defense that allow communication between all the different computers on the Internet.

Telnet is the network terminal protocol that allows you to log on to any other computer on the network anywhere in the world. At Telnet sites, you can only access the information that the site allows you to, unless you already have an account; often university networks work this way, allowing you to access their library information but not much else. As a guest user, from the time you log on to a Telnet site until you finish the session, every character you type is sent directly to the other system just as if you were actually sitting there at that other computer terminal. And all for the price of a local phone call!

Terminal emulation. This is a setting on Telnet computers that allows your computer to translate what the remote Telnet computer is saying. You choose the terminal emulation setting from the menu provided from the Telnet site you are logged on to.

Text simply means *words*. Text is a good example of geek speak.

Threads are discussions within a newsgroup—or mailing list—on a certain topic. Threads are identified by the message header. If you have subscribed to a newsgroup about pets, you may only want to read and reply to the articles about cats.

Trojan. Like the Trojan Horse in Greek mythology, Trojan programs are tiny little programs hidden inside larger regular programs. Like the Trojan warriors, these tiny programs are often hidden there to do nasty things to your computer, like erasing files.

Twit filter. This is a filter in an e-mail program that you use to catch letters from someone you don't want to hear from, or to trash junk e-mail.

UNIX™ is a computer language that was developed by AT&T and is used on many educational computers. Many computer sites on the Internet run under the UNIX™ operating system.

Upload. When you upload you are sending information from your computer to another computer, usually through a modem.

URLs—or Universal Resource Locators—are addresses for the location of any type of Internet resource, whether it is a single file on an FTP site, an entire Gopher server, or an image on the Web. URLs do all of this without you having to know the exact address of where you are, or even how you got there! Note that URLs are case sensitive, which means that uppercase letters are considered different from lowercase letters; *Library*, with a capital "L," is not the same as *library* with a small "l." So be careful when typing in URL addresses.

Usenet is a collection of newsgroups devoted to particular interests of a group of people. Newsgroups might discuss the environment or the latest movie gossip. There's a Usenet newsgroup for almost any topic you can imagine—and if there is a topic *you'd* like to discuss, you can start a new Usenet newsgroup.

User name. That's the name you use to log on to a network. Usually someone has given you permission to log onto the network and has recorded your user name in the network's databank. That way other users can check to find out when you are actively using the network.

Utility programs. These are special little programs to help you keep your computer running the way you want it to. Think of these programs like the tools in your parents' toolbox; you may not use those tools all the time, but when something needs fixing in a hurry, you sure are glad to have them!

Veronica. Veronica is a search tool that you can access through your Gopher program. Veronica allows you to quickly scan Gopherspace for particular files and directories.

Virtual community is any group or gathering that exists in cyberspace. It might be a BBS, a hacking group, a network, or even a *zaibatsu*.

Virtual Reality (VR) is a world that exists only in cyberspace. Modern day virtual reality uses helmets, gloves, and body suits connected to computers that allow you to experience computer-created sensations. Once online you can walk around three-dimensional objects, move things, and communicate with other users through your keyboard. A goal of some VR researchers is to generate a completely alternate reality. The possibilities of VR-generated environments are as limitless as the imagination.

Virtual tourist. Being a virtual tourist simply means visiting places in cyberspace without having to physically go there. You go there online and in your imagination.

WAIS. Wide-Area Information Search is another program for zeroing in on information hidden inside

Gopherspace. You give a WAIS a search word and it scans the Net looking for places where your search word is mentioned. When you start a WAIS, the program will give you a list of which databases you can search. You can select one or more databases for your search. WAIS will then give you a menu of documents, each ranked according to which document best fits your criteria. A "score" of 1,000 is given to the document that contains the most occurrences of your search word. A document with a score of 500 would contain only half as many occurrences.

Web browsers. These are programs that let you navigate through the World Wide Web and see graphics and text on your computer screen. They also allow you to make hypertext leaps to other Web sites. The first Web browser was called Mosaic™, and is still one of the most popular Web browsers at the time this book was published. There are many other Web browser software programs, and when you sign up to get onto the Net, the company you sign up with usually sends you a Web browser software program to get started.

Wildcard. Like the joker in a deck of playing cards, a wildcard is used in a computer search. Usually a wildcard is represented by an *. For instance, *go** means that the search will find every word that starts with *go* and ends with anything, such as *go, going, got, golf,* etc. You have to be careful using wildcards in searches or you'll end up finding a lot of things you weren't looking for. You usually use a wildcard if you don't have the subject of your search narrowed down yet.

World Wide Web. The Web is not the only service on the Internet, but it's rapidly becoming one of the most popular. It's got pictures and hypertext that allow you to jump from one place to another, all over the world, with a single click of a mouse.

Zaibatsu is a Japanese term used by the cyberspace writer, William Gibson. It refers to a large, mega-corporation that owns many other smaller corporations and businesses.

Index of Terms

Acronyms, 31–34, 132, 175

Address, 9, 27, 28, 44, 48, 49, 50–62, 71, 74, 76, 77, 83, 84, 89, 92, 94, 102, 110, 121, 123, 124, 172, 175, 180, 184, 194

America Online, 41, 42, 151, 153, 159, 169, 178, 191

Animation, 127, 143

Apple, 134, 135, 156

Archie, 86, 88–90, 91, 175

Articles, 29, 66, 68, 104, 134, 176, 180, 194

Artificial Reality, 176

ASCII, 77, 78, 176

Batman, 142

Baud, 160, 176

Baud Rate, 176

BBS, See **Bulletin Board System**

Bees, 118, 126

Binary, 64, 65, 77, 78, 176, 177

Bit, 78, 176, 177

Bookmark, 80, 85, 177, 184

Boot up, 23, 177

Bounce, 177

Bulletin Board System, 2, 29, 33, 42, 61, 66, 86, 103, 121, 153, 172, 176, 177, 182, 191, 193

Byte, 78, 88, 176, 177, 182

CERN, 35, 120

CERT, 177

Chat, 6, 10, 24, 25, 26, 28, 63, 69–73, 86, 101, 102, 118, 124, 155, 172, 177, 191

Chat groups, 28

Click on, 36, 37, 38, 49, 54, 56, 58, 82, 83, 178

Command line, 178

Commercial service, 41–43, 44, 48, 52, 53, 56, 64, 86, 141, 151, 152–157, 159, 160, 169, 171, 178

CompuServe, 41, 42, 151, 153–154, 159, 160, 169, 178, 182

Computer language, 42, 178, 194

Computer problems, 135, 143

Cursor, 23, 95, 96, 152, 178, 187

Cybercops, 171, 178, 179 Also see **Datacops**

Cyberian, 178

Cyberpunk, 178, 187

Cyberspace, 1, 2, 3, 5, 12, 16, 17, 18, 19, 21, 23, 24, 25, 28, 40, 45, 50, 60, 66, 69, 79, 80, 83, 87, 93, 101, 102, 103, 104, 105, 107, 108, 109, 110, 117, 118, 126, 132, 150, 168, 169, 170, 171, 172, 174, 175, 177, 178, 181, 182, 183, 185, 188, 191, 193, 195, 197

Darpanet, 19

Data, 48, 57, 86, 127, 178, 179, 181, 183, 188

Database, 36, 38, 46, 73, 74, 88, 90, 92, 93, 130, 141, 152, 175, 179, 196

Datacops, 178, 179

Deck cowboys, 179

Delphi, 42, 151, 154–155, 178

Delurking, 179

Digital, 17, 21, 44, 179, 181

Directory, 73, 77, 78, 84, 88, 90, 91, 179, 188, 189

Disk drive, 47, 48, 50, 179, 180, 181, 183

Document, 36, 38, 39, 57, 62, 76, 79, 80, 82, 83, 84, 86, 88, 89, 90, 91, 92, 122, 180, 181, 183, 184, 190

Domain, 49, 51, 52, 53, 54, 65, 180

Dot, 48, 180

Down, 180

Download, 37, 42, 58, 62, 64, 65, 66, 74, 75, 76, 77, 78, 83, 86, 88, 104, 128, 133, 135, 137, 138, 140, 152, 177, 180, 191

Dweeb, 71, 72, 180

E-mail, 5, 8, 9, 12, 24, 25, 26, 28, 29, 30, 31, 33, 42, 43, 44, 46, 48, 54, 55–60, 61, 63, 68, 71, 72, 73, 86, 89, 90, 93, 94, 102, 103, 104, 105, 110, 129, 132, 133, 153, 154, 155, 156, 158, 160, 170, 171, 177, 178, 180, 191, 192, 194

Emoticons, 32, 192

Encyclopedia, 141

Escape character, 75, 180

eWorld, 42, 151, 156, 178

Exploratorium, 128

FAQ, 33, 61, 62, 66, 103, 132, 138, 141, 142, 180

Feeb, 181

Fiber Optic, 19, 20, 21, 181, 188

File, 8, 28, 36, 38, 42, 48, 55, 58, 59, 61, 62, 63, 64, 65, 66, 67, 70, 76, 77, 78, 80, 83, 84, 86, 88, 90, 91, 103, 105, 118, 126, 127, 132, 135, 136, 138, 152, 154, 157, 170, 174, 175, 176, 177, 179, 180, 181, 182, 185, 188, 189, 190, 191, 194, 195

File Transfer Protcol (FTP), 36, 48, 69, 76–78, 83, 84, 86, 88–90, 105, 110, 118, 128, 130, 132, 135, 136, 153, 154, 155, 160, 175, 176, 181, 182, 189, 191, 194

Filter, 56, 57, 103, 104, 181, 194

Flaming, 70, 101, 103, 104, 105, 170, 171, 181

Floppy disk, 47, 48, 50, 179, 181, 183

Floppy drive, 47, 50, 180, 181

Forum, 103, 104 ,152, 154, 155, 157, 170, 181

Freenet, 121, 122, 182

Freeware, 70, 105, 121, 182, 191

FTP, See **File Transfer Protcol**

Games, 2, 11, 16, 18, 26, 34, 39, 40, 46, 63, 95, 118, 136–137, 142–146, 153, 185, 187

Gateway, 19, 42, 43, 49, 50, 51, 53, 54, 56, 57, 58, 86, 128, 151, 159, 160, 161–165, 169, 171, 178, 182, 184, 191, 192

Gateway server, 42–44, 53, 57, 182

Geek, 17, 182

Geek speak, 17, 182, 193

Getting Online, 41–50, 150–160

GIF, 182

Gigabyte, 88, 182

Gopher, 36, 37, 38, 79, 80, 81, 82, 86, 90, 91, 94, 95, 110, 118, 123, 124, 130, 131, 133, 160, 177, 182, 195

Gopher server, 79, 80, 83, 84, 85, 86, 90, 182, 194

Gopherspace, 78, 79, 80, 81, 82, 83, 86, 90, 91, 92, 94, 182, 195, 196

Graphical browser, 122, 183

Graphical sites, 117, 183

Graphics, 36, 42, 136, 153, 156, 183, 191, 196

Hacker, 173, 179, 183

Handshake, 31, 183

Hang, 183

Hard copy, 55, 57, 59

Hard disk, 47, 64, 78, 83, 179, 180, 183

Hard drive, 38, 47, 48, 104, 180, 183

Header, 9, 29, 58, 66, 67, 183

Highlighted, 37, 82, 83, 183

Host, 49, 50, 52, 180, 184

Hotlist, 184

Hyperlink, 33, 35, 82, 84, 183, 184

Hypermedia, 35, 184

Hypertext, 35, 36, 83, 84, 141, 178, 184, 186, 196, 197

HyperText Markup Language, 84, 184

IBM™, 76, 135, 156

Icon, 32, 37, 38, 43, 54, 94, 96, 178, 192

Ident, 184

Identity hacking, 184

Index file, 78, 88, 184, 185

Information Superhighway, 1, 2, 6

Install, 43, 48, 49, 70, 152, 185

Installation program, 43, 44, 48, 49, 152, 185, 191

Interactive, 128, 133, 136, 176, 185

Internaut, 17, 25, 27, 28, 70, 104, 106, 107, 108, 117, 167, 174, 185

Internet, All pages! **Short history of**, 18–20, **Definition of**, 185

Internet contract, 150, 174

IRC, See **Chat** and **Chat groups**

Jet Propulsion Laboratory, 127

Key pals, 24, 25, 30, 56, 185

Key word, 38, 39, 79, 82, 83, 88, 90, 91, 119, 154, 175, 185

Kites, 118, 136

Leased line access, 186

Libraries, 9, 10, 11, 19, 36, 37, 38, 39, 51, 74, 75, 76, 77, 80, 81, 84, 95, 118, 120, 128, 129, 131, 140–141, 152, 178, 182, 190, 193

Links, 19, 36, 83, 117, 120, 121, 122, 127, 129, 131, 138, 183, 186, 188

Listserver, 28, 29, 60, 186

Listserver mailing list, 28, 61–62, 86, 186

Log off, 24, 59, 78, 102, 186

Log on, 18, 24, 40, 41, 47, 49, 54, 56, 69, 70, 73, 75, 76, 77, 78, 86, 118, 129, 172, 186, 189, 193, 195

Loop, 75, 180, 186

Louvre, 132–133

Lurking, 73, 102, 179, 187

Macintosh™, 41, 42, 49, 65, 69, 76, 156, 158, 160

Mainframe, 19, 73, 187, 192

Microsoft™, 135, 156

MILNET, 19

Modem, 20, 42, 44, 49, 50, 54, 73, 86, 135, 160, 168, 176, 177, 180, 183, 186, 187, 189, 194

Mouse, 6, 23, 24, 35, 36, 38, 40, 49, 50, 54, 78, 82, 83, 89, 96, 178, 183, 184, 187, 189, 197

MUD, 11, 39–40, 187

Museums, 9, 25, 128, 129, 130, 132, 133

NASA, 118, 127, 128, 129

Net, See **Internet**

Netiquette, 138, 143, 187

Netscape™, 41, 43, 122, 157, 159

Network, 2, 6, 10, 19, 20, 21, 28, 37, 39, 42, 44, 48, 53, 54, 74, 121, 143, 170, 177, 179, 185, 188, 190, 193, 195

Newbie, 17, 18, 104, 109, 174, 188

Newspapers, 28, 95, 110, 121, 133–134, 159, 180, 183

Newsreader, 63, 65, 66, 104, 188

Newsgroup, 28, 29, 60, 61, 62, 63, 64, 65, 66, 67, 73, 83, 106, 118, 132, 136, 141–146

NNTP, 36, 37, 188

NSF, 188

NSFNet, 19, 188

Offline, 7, 20, 58, 59, 66, 102, 103, 104, 188

Ohnosecond, 188

Online, 2, 8, 9, 10, 11, 17, 18, 20, 25, 29, 35, 37, 39, 40, 41, 42, 43, 44, 45, 46, 47, 51, 54, 58, 63, 64, 66, 67, 69, 70, 72, 73, 74, 79, 90, 101, 102, 103, 104, 105, 110, 117, 118, 119, 121, 123, 132, 133, 134, 136, 137, 140, 141, 142, 150, 151, 152, 153, 156, 157, 158, 159, 160, 161, 168, 169, 170, 171, 172, 173, 174, 177, 178, 181, 182, 186, 188, 191, 195

Paleontology, 129

Password, 7, 20, 21, 22, 49, 75, 77, 102, 134, 189

Paste, 66, 67, 189

Peripheral, 189

Photography, 118, 130

Ping, 189

POP, 56, 57, 189

Port, 123, 162, 163, 164, 165, 189

PPP, 43, 44, 189, 191

Prodigy, 41, 42, 151, 155–156, 159, 160, 178

Prompt, 189

Protocol, 37, 43, 48, 52, 57, 76, 84, 154, 162–165, 175, 181, 182, 189, 190, 191, 192, 193

PSI, 56, 152, 155–156, 159

Public domain, 64, 65, 189

Readme files, 78, 189

Real time, 69, 70, 86, 177, 190

Remote computer, 11, 20, 24, 41, 73, 74, 75, 76, 77, 78, 83, 86, 118, 186, 190

Ren & Stimpy, 142

Search, 8, 9, 16, 25, 26, 36, 38, 39, 77, 78, 79, 80, 81, 86, 88–90, 90–91, 92–93, 95, 96, 119, 121, 122, 140, 145, 175, 182, 183, 190, 195, 196

Search engine, 38, 39, 78, 80, 90, 93, 182, 190

Search word, 88, 91, 92, 190, 196

Sega, 136, 144

Server, 28, 36, 37, 42, 49, 50, 51, 52, 53, 57, 59, 60, 64, 65, 69, 70, 71, 73, 79, 80, 81, 83, 84, 85, 89, 90, 95, 126, 133, 162–165, 182, 188, 189, 191, 192, 194

Service providers, 150–160

Set up, 36, 43, 47, 48, 54, 56, 58, 59, 70, 74, 77, 79, 152, 191

Shareware, 68, 69, 159, 191

Shell account, 42, 43, 191

Site, 33, 36, 37, 38, 42, 46, 52–53, 58, 69, 73, 75, 77, 78, 83, 84, 88, 90, 91, 94, 105, 110, 117, 122, 118, 119–146, 180, 183, 189, 191, 193, 194, 196

SLIP, 43, 44, 186, 189, 191

SLIP/PPP dial up access, 43, 44, 186, 191

Smiley, 30, 31–34, 192

Smithsonian, 128, 133

SMTP, 57, 192

Software, 6, 9, 10, 21, 36, 41, 43, 44, 46, 47, 48, 49, 54, 57, 65, 75, 76, 78, 82, 88, 103, 118, 127, 133, 134, 135, 142, 144, 152, 153, 157, 158, 160, 175, 178, 179, 181, 182, 184, 185, 188, 189, 191, 192, 196

Spacelink, 129

Space shuttle, 118, 127, 145

SPAM, 67, 192

Sports, 118, 137, 143, 145, 155

Star Trek, 139, 143

Subdomain, 53, 54

Supercomputer, 19, 20, 192

Surfing, 2, 11, 16, 17, 18, 21, 26, 27, 42, 44, 49, 50, 66, 96, 101–106, 107, 143, 154, 157, 168, 173, 174, 178, 186, 187, 193

Sysadmin, 193

Sysop, 34, 103, 193

TCP/IP, 44, 48, 54, 193

Telnet, 48, 73–75, 76, 83, 86, 89, 95, 110, 118, 124, 129, 130, 153, 154, 155, 160, 193

Terminal emulation, 74, 75, 193

Text, 193

Thread, 29, 66, 136

Tools, See E-mail, Chat, FTP, Gopher, IRC, Telnet, Usenet

Transfer, 37, 50, 64, 76–78, 86, 154, 176, 181, 182, 183, 188, 192

Twit filter, 103, 194

UNIX™, 42, 69, 178, 191, 194

Upload, 194

URL, 83, 84, 123, 194

Usenet, 29, 37, 62, 63–68, 83, 86, 110, 118, 132, 136, 141, 142–146, 154, 158, 160, 188, 194

User name, 20, 21, 24, 51, 52, 53, 74, 162–165, 189, 195

Utility program, 105, 195

Veronica, 79, 80, 86, 90–91, 195

Virtual community, 195

Virtual Reality, 40, 145, 176, 195

Virtual tourist, 24, 195

WAIS, 86, 91, 92, 195–196

Web, See World Wide Web

Web browser, 9, 36, 82, 83, 86, 93, 121, 153, 155, 157, 196

Web crawler, 92

Wildcard, 89, 196

Windows™, 41, 69, 135, 158, 160

World Wide Web, 2, 9, 33, 35–36, 37, 38, 42, 81, 82–85, 86, 92–93, 106, 110, 117–146, 153, 154, 155, 157, 158, 160, 177, 183, 184, 196, 197

X-Files, 138

Zaibatsu, 195, 197

NOTES

NOTES

NOTES

NOTES

NOTES

NOTES

NOTES

NOTES

NOTES

NOTES

ABOUT THE AUTHORS

Ted Pedersen has been involved in computers since he was a programmer in Seattle. Although he switched to full-time writing several years ago, he has continued to be a computer consultant for various companies and studios. Ted has written for children's television, most recently developing the new *Skysurfer Strike Force* animated series. He is also co-author of the new high-tech Internet series of *Cybersurfers* novels for Price Stern Sloan, and the author of two *Deep Space Nine* young adult books. In addition to his book and TV projects, he is currently writing his first interactive game. Ted and his wife, Phyllis, share their home in Venice, California with several cats and computers.

Francis Moss has written more than 100 animated TV scripts and has been a story editor on the *Teenage Mutant Turtles* and *James Bond, Jr.* series. His nonfiction children's book, *Dangerous Animals*, will be published in 1996. As a computer user, he has been actively surfing the Internet and has been a beta tester for new programs, including Microsoft's Windows 95™. Francis and his wife, Phyllis, live in North Hollywood, California, with their two children, Zachary and Caitlin, one dog, two cats, and three computers.